# Briarcliff Manor

# Briarcliff Manor

## A NOVEL

*SHARON ANNE SALVATO*

STEIN AND DAY/*Publishers*/New York

First published in 1974
Copyright © 1974 Sharon Salvato
Library of Congress Catalog Card No. 73-90701
All rights reserved
Designed by David Miller
Printed in the United States of America
Stein and Day/*Publishers*/Scarborough House, Briarcliff Manor, N.Y. 10510
ISBN 0-8128-1661-7

# Briarcliff Manor

# 1

I AM NOT CONSIDERED pretty, and never have been. Even as a child I knew this. While other children were held in arms so the adoring eyes of visitors could better behold their rosy cheeks and smiling faces, I was sitting primly on a chair in an out-of-the-way corner. No one ever came to fetch me. They would glance over and say, "What a strange little creature she is. Is she always so quiet?"

My father would nod in tacit agreement. He never delved into the subject of me, if at all possible.

I wasn't as miserable as it might have seemed, for I was not aware of the barrenness of my life. All I had ever known was Briarcliff Manor, and the people who made up my "family." The Manor itself was enough to fascinate and tantalize me as a child. Father must have built it anticipating numerous descendants to inhabit it for generations to come. It had been built of native stone, much of it from the banks of the Hudson River that ran along the north boundary of the property. The rock had not been cut smoothly, so Briarcliff Manor rose four full stories out of the ground like a cliff separated from its mountain, alone and unsheltered in the midst of a softly rolling meadow.

It looked both natural and artificial at the same time, and was always special to me as a child, when my time was most happily occupied by dreams of princesses and knights and dragons.

The road that led to Briarcliff Manor was lined with tall birch trees, pale and ghostly, which formed a wood of some density on both sides. I remember how often the dappled sunlight coming through the trees and onto the dusty road lulled me into a dreamlike paradise as the carriage made its way home. The sunbeams became the stars for me, or snowflakes, and sometimes I would imagine I was underwater, and that the lights glimmering on the road were specks of sunlight reaching deep into the dark sea.

There was not a place around the house that was not a favorite of mine for one reason or another. Winters were the bleakest times, for no one could be spared to entertain a child at Briarcliff Manor, and I was confined to the house for the most part. As a consequence the two people who had the greatest influence on me were Aggie, our cook, and Janet, my mother's nurse. It was through them that I learned to be thoroughly competent in running a household. This ability gave me a kind of assurance I lacked in other matters. It is strange how qualities such as usefulness and competence can replace prettiness or even love.

For me these qualities had to suffice. There *was* no love to be found within the walls of Briarcliff Manor. My mother had been taken ill when I was no more than two, or perhaps three. I was never told what happened to her, nor did I ask. It was one of the things we never spoke of. At its core, I sensed, lay the seed of my father's hatred of both my mother and myself. The subject was always a source of fear and confusion for me, so I tried very hard to be like Aggie and Janet, turning away from whatever my mother might have been.

My discretion turned out to be fortunate. Father said it was the only thing that gave him any hope for me. All else about me he loathed. The look of me, he said, was that of a homely child's face matured too soon. My hair was too brown, eyes not brown enough, nose too long and too straight. It seemed that for him I had too much or too little of everything, and I had neither the poise of my own nor the guidance of a woman to help me manage the attributes I possessed.

I was to learn much later that I had a foreign appearance, but as a girl with only my father's opinion to guide me, I cowered and shrank from the critical eyes of anyone who might see me. So many of the people who lived nearby would look on those of us from Briarcliff Manor in a peculiar and curious fashion. I was too young to realize that there might be other reasons for the strange looks than the existence of one awkward young girl.

I was painfully aware of the burden I was to my father. He had to display me to the world, for I could not be hidden away as completely as could my mother. No one was allowed to visit her, except for the doctor, and he did not come frequently. When he did come, he stood at the foot of her bed and just looked at her. I once heard him tell Father that no one could make Mother well but Mother herself. I suppose that was when I knew for certain she would die.

Fortunately Father and I did not see much of each other during those years. He worked incessantly; he was often in a terrible mood and best avoided. The estate is now very large, but during my growing-up years he was still acquiring it. The servants spoke often of the property he bought. I didn't know why, but the general opinion was that he had done something bad in buying the land that made up Briarcliff Manor. This may have been true, for he was very mysterious in his dealings, and there was a man who came to the house often during this time. He and my father had some very nasty arguments about the land and about my mother.

It was right after one of these meetings that my father sent me away.

I had been on my way to the kitchen to see Aggie when I heard the raised voice of my father. He and the man I did not know were coming directly toward me, so I quickly slipped around the corner and hid myself under the stairwell.

"What is it this time? Water again?" my father asked.

"There is no point in talking around the subject, John. We

both know why I'm here. It's always the same, nothing is changed, so we might as well get on with it. Will you let me see her this time?" The man's voice was calm, not excited the way my father's voice was.

"No, you can't see her! We've been over and over this. If that's all you want, get out of here."

"She's going to die, you know that. We're running out of time. For God's sake give me a chance—you can't refuse like that, I'm only asking to see her for a few moments. Ten minutes. Give me that, just ten minutes."

"Get *out* of here!"

I knew they were talking about my mother. No one else, except me, could cause such an angry reaction in Father.

"I not only can refuse you, but I will have it no other way. Let her die, she's been dead to me for years."

"Once, John, let me see her once. Only the ten minutes I asked for—no more, I give you my word. I will leave here then, I promise. I'll never come near Briarcliff Manor again."

"What makes you think you have a choice? You have no bargaining power with me. You are not to see her, and you will not be on my property. I don't want her alive, can't you get that through your head? I wait for the day she dies. I won't be run to the ground, humiliated, made a laughingstock by her. So go on, get off Briarcliff land just as you said, and don't bother to come back. You were right when you said time was running out—it has run out for you!"

The man stood looking at Father. He didn't seem to know what to say, and I hoped he wouldn't say anything else. He looked like a nice man, and I wanted him to leave quickly before anything happened.

"It's the same as murder. You've already deprived her of years of fruitful life," I heard the man say in his strange deep, soft voice. My father laughed.

"And you, her guardian angel, will breathe new life into her."

"Let me try."

"No."

"If I turned my farm over to you, and you owned all of the

10

original tract—would you make a bargain for her life with me then?"

"Now you look here, you damned bleeding heart, who are you to come to me with a proposition like that? You don't have any land without me, and don't you forget it. You haven't water. Look at your fields—go look at them. Dried-out scrub grass, not fit to graze sheep on. I don't need your bargains. You may not know it, but I have your land now. I have only to wait until you hand over the deed."

"Not this time, John. I'd give that property away before I'd let you have it."

"Who would take it? No one will defy me. You have over-reached yourself, you know. There are things you should have considered before you came here to make bargains with me about my wife."

"What happened was years ago, John. You've punished her enough . . . and me. Isn't my word to never see her again enough?"

"You make me sick with that prattle, and your sanctimonious looks. If you want to get to the truth, look at it straight—it's you who are killing her, not I. It's your sin, not mine. If I ever see your face again I'll shoot you. I'll leave your damned body in the ditch to rot. Now get out of here. Get out!"

The man left. He looked very sad, but my father looked worse. His face was blotched, and red marks showed through his beard. I had never seen him in as bad a temper as he was in that day.

When he came down the hall, he walked right past me. I made myself as small as I could beneath the stairwell.

I waited for what seemed a long time until I could no longer hear his footsteps, then I ran to the kitchen. Aggie was there, and I wanted to be near her. She gave me a glass of fresh milk, still warm from the cow's body. I drank it as though I had never before had a glass of milk, and I ate all of the little cakes she put before me.

We all started when we heard my father's voice. He didn't use the bell pull to ask for what he wished, but yelled in his very deep, loud voice.

"Annabel! Annabel!"

"You'd better hurry on and see what he wants, miss," Aggie said.

"I don't want to go," I told her. "He is very angry, Aggie. I don't want to go."

"Poor lamb! But it's always worse when he can't find you. Hurry on now and see what he wants."

"He is angry because some man came and talked to him about Mother this morning. Who was he, Aggie? Why did he make Father so upset?"

"Never you mind about the man, now. You get yourself upstairs as quick as you can. Come here, let me straighten you a bit. Remember, be your prettiest for him. This has nothing to do with you—remember that. He's not really angry with you."

Aggie was kind, and she was usually right.

I had just started to get up, when Janet came into the kitchen.

"Oh, there you are—come quickly! He wants you, and he's in a state."

Janet looked very pale. Next to me, I think she was more frightened of my father than anyone else in the house.

"I am ready," I said in a voice I thought to be very brave.

She took my hand and we went upstairs to my father's sitting room. Janet told me to sit there until he called me into the small study he kept adjoining his rooms.

Right then, I knew for certain that my life was about to change. I was forbidden to go near Father's small study, and had never seen the inside of it. He never asked anyone to meet him there except servants who were to be dismissed.

I did not know what the stranger had meant with all of his talk about my mother. I knew nothing of the land he spoke of, nor did I know why he seemed so important to my father. But I did know what it meant to be called to the upstairs study.

I waited for a long time. Father's chair was too tall for me, and I had to sit very straight with my feet dangling awkwardly in the air. My legs felt all prickly by the time he called to me. When I entered the room he was sealing a letter.

"This," he waggled the letter in my face, "is a letter to Miss Eugenia Hamilton. Do you know who she is, Annabel?"

12

"No, Father. I don't believe you have ever mentioned her to me before."

"She runs a school for girls. She makes ladies of them, so we shall see what, if anything, she can do with you."

Father was always thinking of ways to make me more tolerable. I think he liked pretty little curly-headed girls, because he always seemed happy when our neighbor Mrs. Hollander brought her daughter Nancy to our house. She had blond hair that made little ringlets all around her face, and she smiled all the time.

"Am I to be like Nancy Hollander?" I asked him, thinking that I wouldn't much care for that in spite of his approval of her.

He looked at me seriously for a moment. "I don't believe we can expect that much change, but she will make you a presentable young lady. At least, she will try."

"I will have to leave Briarcliff Manor."

"Of course."

"Father, I don't want to leave."

"You will begin in the fall."

His words were calm, but his face had begun to get red again. Father could tolerate me only in small doses, and I should have known that he was exerting great restraint with me this morning. I had expected a terrible scene with him, and he was being quite calm. But I could not help myself. I didn't want to leave. I was afraid he might never allow me to return.

"I don't want to go."

"Annabel! There is no question. You are going, and I want you fully prepared to accept what Miss Hamilton has to offer."

"Will I ever get to come back home?"

"That will depend. We shall discuss it later . . . when we see how you progress." His eyes glittered, and I felt he wanted to laugh at me and was keeping it inside.

There was nothing to do but to follow his wishes. Several times during the summer I tried to talk to him about the subject, but he would not answer me.

The day I left for Miss Hamilton's, Janet came to take me to see my mother. On normal days I was allowed in the room only at special times, but Janet felt an exception could be made as I was leaving and would not see Mother for a long time.

It was not something I wanted to do, for I had never been able to think of Mother as a person. She didn't know who I was, or even that I was there. She was just a part of Briarcliff that I accepted as I did any other.

I was taken to see her once each morning and once before bed each night. Father visited her on schedule too. I don't know if the schedules were made for the benefit of the nurse—they may have been—but I truly believe they were made so Father would never find himself in the same room with Mother and me together.

On the day I was to leave for school we had missed my morning visit. Janet insisted I should see Mother before I left.

"You never know, Annabel, when she may open her eyes and see you. We must help her by being there. Wouldn't you like your mother to be well again?"

"Oh, yes, I do want her well! But, Janet, she is always the same—she never sees me. Not ever."

"Never you mind. We mustn't give up, must we?"

I followed her dutifully into the room. I did want my mother well, but I hated standing beside her bed. Janet said I must talk to her just as though she were listening, and I never knew what to say. I was self-conscious and aware of Janet standing by and listening to me.

"Hello, Mother," I said to the figure on the bed. "I came to visit you. I am going away. Father is sending me to Miss Eugenia Hamilton's school, but—Janet, *why* do I have to talk to her? See? She isn't listening."

Janet did not get a chance to reply, for the door opened and my father came in. I thought he looked like a giant; he seemed to fill the doorway with his body. I backed away from the bed, trying to make myself invisible. His hair was wiry and black, and he never smiled. On this day he looked hideous, with great lines carved into his face by his mouth. I was certain he would never let me come home. He wanted to be rid of me. He hated me as much as he hated my mother.

He had frightened Janet too, for when he entered she took several steps back, as I had.

"What is she doing in here? This is no time for the child to be around."

"I am sorry, sir," Janet stammered. "She won't be seeing her mother for so long . . . I thought you would want her to see Mrs. Arbriar before she left this afternoon."

"Well, I don't, and I don't pay you to think. Your job begins and ends with that." He raised his great arm and pointed at my mother.

I had been carefully edging my way toward Janet, hoping she wouldn't leave before I could get to her side.

"Move!" my father shouted at her. "Get out of here, and take her with you."

She reached out and took my hand. We both scurried out of the room as fast as we could.

"Don't cry, little one. I'm sure he doesn't mean a half of what he says."

But I wasn't crying, and I knew that he meant all that he said.

I went to Miss Hamilton's school that afternoon. I did not return to Briarcliff Manor for four years, and saw my father only at special holidays and visiting days at the school.

I had just passed my fourteenth birthday the month before I entered the school, and I was young for my age. Most often I was taken to be no more than ten, partly due to my lack of height and partly because I had been very sheltered at Briarcliff Manor. Until I arrived at Miss Hamilton's I had thought the Manor's atmosphere a normal one. I was to learn much during my years away from home.

2

MISS HAMILTON DID NOT remind me of any teacher I had ever seen before. She was a kind lady, plump and fashionable, and gave the impression of being completely relaxed and entertained at all times. It was not until my father announced that we were not there for a visit, but that I was to remain behind and begin my schooling immediately, that the slightest crack in her serenity showed. She had not expected me for at least another week, and no room was prepared for me. I was led to a sitting room to wait while she made arrangements for me.

"That didn't take too long, did it, Miss Arbriar? We have a nice room for you. I am sure you will be comfortable."

I knew I would be miserable wherever she put me, but I couldn't very well say so.

"I know I shall, Miss Hamilton."

"Come, now, let's not have a long face on our first day here. You may consider this your first lesson. A lady does not let her emotions show in her carriage or demeanor. It spoils her looks, and it is death to her socially. No one, certainly no gentleman, wants to be burdened with a sour-looking young lady."

"Yes, Miss Hamilton."

I wished she would hurry me to my room. I was about to

cry, and I was certain that if I did this in her presence I would receive my second lesson in being a lady.

I followed her up the long uncarpeted flight of stairs. My feet made much more noise on the wooden steps than hers did. I looked down to see if she really had feet. I knew at that moment Father would be disappointed, for I should never be able to walk like Miss Hamilton. I walked like Aggie.

"This floor," she said, turning at the second landing, "is customarily for the older girls, but since you have arrived early Sue Ellen Marks has graciously offered herself as your roommate."

"That was nice of her. Is she very much older than I?"

"You are fourteen, are you not?"

I nodded, and she frowned.

"Well, she would be two years older than you. That is not so much, although one would never suspect that you are fourteen."

We went into a large green room with high ceilings and long narrow windows. Sue Ellen's things were in great evidence. I thought it fortunate that I had few possessions other than my clothes, for there would not have been space for them.

Miss Hamilton was giving me instruction as to what was expected of me, and where I was to come at eight o'clock when we had supper. She finally left me, and I forgot all that she had said. I flung myself across the hard bed, crying, longing for the soft feathers and eiderdown of my bed at Briarcliff Manor, which Aggie kept fresh and smelling like the sun beating down on freshly mown grass.

It was in this state that Sue Ellen found me when she returned to her room. I did not know she had entered until she spoke.

"The first few days are terrible, aren't they? It's awful to have to leave home, but don't worry, you will like it better soon."

I jumped up and did my best to quickly wipe the tears from my face.

"Are you the girl I am to share the room with?"

"No, I am the *lady* who is willing to share her room with you!"

18

Sue Ellen had dancing blue eyes, and she was born a tease, but I didn't know it that first awful day.

"I'm sorry," I said, the tears starting again. "I didn't mean to be presumptuous. It is *kind* of you to let me share your room."

"My goodness! You really are in a state. Maybe you are given to the vapors. That would be exciting—a roommate with vapors."

She cocked her head to one side to see if there was any chance of my succumbing to total melancholia on the spot.

"I am not given to the vapors," I said with a little more force.

"Oh, well, never mind. There will be something else to make you interesting. You must know it is imperative I have a reason for allowing you to be my roommate. It's a privilege, you know. I couldn't bear it if the other girls thought you were *pushed* on me by Miss Hamilton! That would be too humiliating."

"I don't see what is so bad about having me as a roommate."

"You're fourteen," she said as though it were a crime. "I am sixteen years old, and it is as plain as the nose on your face that you are completely green. Probably this is your first time away from home. I shall be humiliated beyond endurance—I just know it."

She flopped down on the bed, her feet out in front of her in a fashion that would warrant a lesson in ladyship from Miss Hamilton.

"I shall try not to embarrass you any more than I can help. I am good at staying out of the way."

"You'll never become a lady if you hide yourself all the time. Your papa would just be wasting his money if that was all you did."

"Then what shall I do?'"

"I don't know. We shall have to think about it at great length. I forget your name. Miss Hamilton said it too fast."

"Annabel Arbriar."

"Annabel—that's a pretty name. Well, Annabel, I think we will become good friends . . . I think."

I was surprised at her words, as I thought she looked upon

me as a burden she would have to suffer. But she turned out to be right, after all, and we did become fast friends.

I must give Sue Ellen all the credit for that friendship as well as for my moderate success at Miss Hamilton's. Had it not been for her unconquerably sunny nature, I would have failed miserably, and no doubt been returned ignominiously to Briarcliff Manor. It didn't take me long to render Miss Hamilton into a condition of near-despair at the futility of her efforts to improve me.

One afternoon, about six months after I had come to the school, the dressmaker came to make our spring frocks. Each girl was to have a decisive part in the selection of material, design, and color, so that we would be well versed in fashion. I had not been able to overcome my long-standing habit of making myself as inconspicuous as possible. I had always worn gray, brown, and fawn colors at Briarcliff Manor, and I chose these for my new dresses.

"Whatever is this!" Miss Hamilton exclaimed as she saw the drab materials, each designed to be serviceable for at least ten years, displayed before me.

"You can't mean *these* are the fabrics you wish to have made up for you?"

As usual I had no grasp on my newly acquired poise. I stood stammering, wondering what I had done wrong this time.

"My dear, this is impossible. We are selecting these frocks for spring—light, gay, young colors are the thing. You couldn't possibly consider being seen in these." She looked down at the patterns that lay near the material.

"But I don't know what else to choose, Miss Hamilton!"

She motioned to Mrs. Hendricks, the seamstress, who rummaged through a gargantuan bag stuffed with patterns and designs.

"Virtually anything would be better than what you have selected, but look at these. Aren't there any that suit you? I can't believe a girl would deliberately choose to look like a scullery maid." Miss Hamilton threw one more discouraged look at my selections.

The ones she handed to me were decorated with lace and inset panels. They were beautiful, and I longed for them.

"I couldn't wear these," I said simply.

"Why ever not? Your father has not stipulated any limitations on your funds; they are attractive fabrics. I can't imagine why you can't wear them."

"They are too pretty for me."

Her hand immediately flew up to her brow. She closed her eyes a moment as if gathering strength from beyond.

"Annabel! You have learned nothing. No lady would ever say a dress is too pretty for her. Never! Where have you acquired these ideas?"

She turned to Mrs. Hendricks. "Do what you can with this child." Once more she looked at me, her eyes critical. Her dainty hand came out and touched my waist. "Accentuate the long line of her waist; it will give her a graceful, lithe look."

She turned me around, first this way, then that, both she and Mrs. Hendricks clucking over my strong points and shortcomings. "She has good lines, if we could ever convince her to leave off wearing these atrocious costumes of hers. You know what is suitable, Mrs. Hendricks; pick the patterns and some materials that will make her look attractive. Perhaps that will make her feel more as she should about herself, although I am about to despair that anything shall. Lord knows nothing else has penetrated her mind." Once again she daintily placed her hand to her forehead.

"I will do my best, Miss Hamilton. I think you can trust me to provide a few happy surprises for you and the young lady."

"Oh, do try. I am past knowing what to do with Annabel's retiring ways. I shudder to think what Mr. Arbriar will say when he sees we have been able to accomplish so little with his daughter. The reputation of this school will be in ruins. Go to your room, Annabel. I shall talk to you when I am better able to think."

I gave her a wobbling curtsy and hurried to my room. She did indeed talk to me later, and I promised to try to think beautifully. She was sure that would help, and indeed it did, as long as she required me only to think and not act. The new and beautiful dresses that arrived with a cheerful, encouraging note from Mrs. Hendricks hung unused in my wardrobe.

One evening early in the spring we were to come to dinner

dressed in gowns. It was a special night, and Miss Hamilton told me that I was to wear one of the new gowns or I would be sent to my room. I spent the afternoon trying to find one that would not make me feel conspicuous.

"What are you going to wear tonight?" Sue Ellen asked as soon as she came into the room.

"I don't know. Miss Hamilton said I couldn't stay downstairs unless I wore one of the gowns she had made for me. Do you think she would really send me upstairs if I wore the gray?"

"Ninny! Everyone would think you were the serving girl. Why don't you wear the pink lacy one?"

"No! I couldn't."

"Why not?"

"It's too pretty."

"That's the best reason I know *for* wearing it."

"But people would think I was drawing attention to myself. I couldn't do that, I would die of embarrassment. They would laugh at me."

Sue Ellen sat down, much more attentive now, and she looked at me as though she was seeing me for the first time.

"What kind of a home did you come from, Annabel? What did they do to you—hasn't anyone ever told you you're beautiful?"

I wished my father had been there to hear her say that. It would have pleased me to have him know that someone approved of my looks. I thought of the other person who had expressed liking for my appearance, and quickly I told Sue Ellen.

"One person thought I was beautiful, but I don't know if you would count him . . . my father didn't."

"Why not? Who was he?"

"Well, he loved me, you see. I would be pretty to him, because . . . well, because he did love me, and he was foreign, and he thought unusual looks agreeable."

"Well, who was he?"

"It was Jules, our head groom at Briarcliff Manor, and he thought I looked like Nefertiti. She was a queen, but that doesn't count either, because when I looked at her, she was just a statue with a long neck and looked very proud."

"I've seen pictures of the statue too," Sue Ellen said as she eyed me up and down. "I think he is right."

"I wish he were. Jules is wonderful. He taught me how to ride when my father said I would have to wait. He taught me to jump a horse, too."

"Was he handsome, and in love with you?'"

I couldn't help but giggle when I thought of Jules like that. "No," I said. "He is old, older than my father, and he has wrinkles all over. But he was wonderful, and he gave me my horse. Do you remember I told you about Bucephalus? Well, it was Jules who named him. Bucephalus was the horse of Alexander the Great, and Jules said I could not have a lesser horse than one that belonged to a king."

"I think I would like Jules," Sue Ellen said, picking at the edge of the coverlet. "But I don't think I would like your father."

She looked up to see if I was angry. I was not, though the comment *had* surprised me.

"Father is a respected man," I said. "I have never heard anyone say they didn't like him. Everyone does just what he says."

"Yes, I know, or I mean I guessed that, but—haven't you ever wondered why? Oh, never mind. It isn't nice to say things like that to people about their own families. But it does seem, Annabel, that your house is different from any other I've ever heard about. It seems to be full of all kinds of secrets, and then your father hating everybody . . . well, *why* would everyone be afraid of him, and why would you be afraid for people to notice you, and to see how pretty you are? I don't think you should ever go back there, Annabel, not ever."

I had no answer for Sue Ellen. I had never looked back upon my home from a distance before, or through anyone else's eyes.

I had always known that I felt more secure when I could melt into the background, and thought it was because my own person was so unattractive that I was such a burden, but

23

perhaps I had been wrong. Perhaps those feelings I had were simply fear. I didn't know what had happened to my mother. I didn't know who the stranger was that my father hated, and I didn't know why Father disliked me as he did. I didn't know why the servants whispered about him, then stopped as soon as I came near. I knew nothing except that I liked to stay away from the center of things. Sue Ellen was right. I was, and had been most of my life, afraid. But I didn't know what it was that I feared.

I had become lost in my thoughts and visions of Briarcliff Manor, but Sue Ellen went on in her cheerful and practical way, searching through my gowns.

"Wear this one, Annabel," she pleaded. "It is so exotic, and it will make your hair look dark and lovely. You will be just like Jules said you are." She held up a larkspur-colored silk, and I did wear it.

I do not know if it was the gown, as Miss Hamilton thought, or Sue Ellen's words about Briarcliff Manor, but in some ways that night began a new life for me. My poise kept slipping away from me, and I was still awkward at times, but for the first time I began to see myself as something other than an extension of Briarcliff Manor, yet another one of my father's possessions.

I never went back to the drab clothes I had brought from home. I never became Miss Hamilton's star pupil, but never again did she look upon me in despair. It was four years before I returned to Briarcliff Manor. Sue Ellen and I parted sadly, she still protesting that I should never return home.

"There is nothing for you there but unhappiness and bitterness, Annabel. Don't go, please don't go. My mother and father would be so happy to have you live with us. Don't go back to Briarcliff Manor. Let your father have it!"

"I can't turn my back on my father and my home, Sue Ellen. And what of my mother? Should I just abandon her? I never understood before, but it is different now. I must go home. And besides, how can I ever be sure of myself if I cannot face my father?"

"I don't know. All your arguments are right, Annabel, but I can't help, I"—her deep-blue eyes were filled with tears as she looked at me—"I *know* you won't be happy at Briarcliff Manor."

I wasn't at all sure she wasn't right, but we parted nevertheless with promises of keeping in touch and visiting each other.

My first taste of the life that awaited me at Briarcliff Manor came when I went to my mother's room. Sue Ellen and I had spoken often of her, and the strangeness of the way my father treated her. It was one of the things I now wanted to change. I was eager to do my best to aid her in coming "back to life," and felt certain that with time and patience this could be accomplished. The doctor had said often that there was no physical reason for her state. It was a matter of despair, and a desire to avoid facing life. I was certain I could deal with that.

When I arrived, I did not notice that Janet was not in the house. I came in the front door and went directly to Mother's room. There I stood, stunned. The room was freshly decorated and cheerful. The bed was empty; nothing stood on the dresser to indicate the presence of an occupant; there were no clothes or paraphernalia about. There was nothing alive about the room at all. Lettie, a new servant, who was to be my personal maid, came up behind me as I stood surveying the room in shock.

"It is a nice room, isn't it, miss? It is one of my favorites . . . so nice and bright like."

"But where is my mother?" I said, not looking at Lettie.

"Mrs. Arbriar? Oh, but surely Miss, you don't mean . . . Surely you know—"

*"Where is my mother?"*

Lettie looked extraordinarily uncomfortable, and moved her feet first this way then that.

"But, miss, *I* shouldn't be tellin' you . . . Not like this."

"Just tell me, please."

"Mrs. Arbriar, miss, well, Mrs. Arbriar has been dead now nearly a year. It happened even before I came to work here."

"A year? My mother has been dead a year?"

Even before Lettie had stammered out her answer I had guessed Mother was dead, but I thought she must have died recently. I was not at all prepared for the possibility that my father had neglected to tell me for such a long time. I had forgotten the cold indifference that was so much a part of him.

When I faced him with my indignant and hurt feelings, he

shrugged and said it made no difference. He would not have permitted me to return to Briarcliff Manor for her funeral, so what would have been the point of upsetting me?

Angry and hurt as I was, I had never been able to face my father and could not then. Sue Ellen had been right. I had learned much at Miss Hamilton's school, but one thing I realized as I adjusted to living again at Briarcliff Manor was that being a lady is in large part dependent upon the respect and good will of those with whom one is dealing. My father refused to see me as anything but a problem, or perhaps as a project which he might yet bring to a successful conclusion. Until my return, I had not been aware of this aspect of father's feelings for me, and I was completely unprepared to handle it.

He meant to marry me to an eligible young man, thereby gaining the son he'd never had *and* a suitable person to run Briarcliff Manor for him. The Manor was an obsession with him, I knew, but I did not know from what he wanted it secure.

To accomplish his purposes Father held a great coming-out ball for me. Looking back on it I can now see that it was almost vulgar in its lavishness. But even that, it seems, served my father's purposes, and I saw the house come alive with unaccustomed excitement. Looking in from the outside, I imagine anyone would have thought we were having the time of our lives. But *I* was once more cowering in fear.

I knew that if ever there was a time when I should have the upper hand over my father, it was at my own coming-out ball. I should be in command to choose and reject whom I pleased. It was for this very moment that Miss Hamilton had spent her patient hours trying to prepare me. But my weeks at home had stripped me of all my precarious self-confidence. I was again the shy, retiring, fearful girl I had been before I went to Miss Hamilton. The only difference was that now I had Sue Ellen to reach out to, and I did. I wrote long soul-searching letters, telling her of my dread of being presented. I told her of Father's driving need to find me securely married, and to a very special kind of husband.

I knew there would be no marriage to a man who could not qualify on Father's first concern, the management of Briarcliff

Manor. I said many prayers, and often thought of the letters I was writing as prayers as well—for I too wanted a husband, but one who would love me. I did not believe that my father would consider my feelings at all, so I prayed for some kind of intervention that would assure us each of what we wished. In a way my prayers were answered, but not as I had anticipated.

George Edgerton was the shining star among the gentlemen that season. I met him the night of my own ball, and though I was struck by him I did not entertain hope for a similar notice from him. He was among the few who noticed the extravagance of our ball, and I thought he would want no part of the Arbriars. Nevertheless, I joined the other girls when they talked of him. He had a place of endearment in every lady's heart, and well he should have. One would have had to be carved from granite not to be taken with a man who looked like the pale golden child of the moon, tall and supple, made to be adored by all who chanced within his orbit.

The night of my "triumph," I had dressed in a shimmering ivory satin gown trimmed in a soft ecru lace. In that dress, even I could not doubt that I looked attractive. On that evening George Edgerton made known his interest in me.

In the beginning I had never dared hope to so much as dance with him, but that had come to pass, and was followed by whole evenings we spent together, and I had doubted those, and now he was asking for my hand. He wanted me for a wife. Silly goose that I was, I hadn't the slightest notion of a husband, or what he should be once he had stepped out of my dream. I floated along in my gossamer world, knowing only that I wanted to be loved and cherished, and George told me fervently that I should never have to doubt again, for he would always be at my side.

The ivory gown I had worn the night George proposed to me was put away lovingly to be taken out again the night of our engagement announcement. For days following the ball I blissfully re-created his proposal, going over each word of promise until I could think of little else. I did not think I could wait for the day he would formally ask for my hand.

When he came to Briarcliff Manor to speak to my father, he

was shown into the library. Father always used that room for business, and my future husband certainly fell into *that* category.

George was in the library for about an hour. I was across the hall, pacing the room and wishing I had the courage to eavesdrop. From the moment he had entered, I barely took my eyes from the door. When it finally opened, I saw that he looked very pleased. Even his walk told me that the conversation had gone to his satisfaction.

I rushed toward him, eager to discuss Father's acceptance of him and the plans for our future. There were so many things I wanted to tell him.

As soon as he saw me coming, his face froze into a mask. Had I not known it was George, I don't believe I would have recognized him. There was none of the grace, the warmth, the charm, that I had come to expect in him. I stopped walking, and watched openmouthed as he turned away from me and went out the door. The door closed softly after him, and I remained glued in place, not able to imagine what had made him change so abruptly.

I envied the girls I had gone to school with. They would have cried or pouted, or stamped their feet, while I could do nothing but look puzzled, and go in search of an explanation. I went to the library.

Father was rolling some brandy around in a small crystal snifter, looking entirely satisfied with himself—much as George had looked when he had first left the room.

"Father, did you and George reach an agreement?"

As he looked up at me, his expression changed.

"Yes. We did."

"And what was that?"

Again he looked up. This time there was no mistaking his expression. His eyes started at the top of my head and moved slowly and meticulously down past my mauve dress to my scuffed but serviceable shoes. My heart fluttered in relief that it was George's standards I had to meet, and not Father's.

I looked back at him. His hair was now the color of iron, and the weight he had added to his already large frame made him seem more massive. His eyes shone with a hardness that made me shrivel within myself when he turned his gaze on me. Finally, his voice came from deep within.

"Didn't George tell you of our agreement?"

"No, Father. George behaved very strangely just now."

"I don't doubt that," he said. "George found that he preferred money in his greedy hands to living a life with you. I don't suppose that ever occurred to you, did it, Annabel? You'd never have guessed a man would offer to marry you to inherit Briarcliff Manor." He laughed to himself, and then added, "I am well rid of him. He never would have been man enough to replace me. I don't imagine I should have expected better from any man you would bring home."

His words summed up his whole feeling about me, and about the matter of George Edgerton. Just as my mother had failed, so had I. Neither of us had given Father his heir.

For some reason, losing George did not bother me as much as the idea that I might be desirable only becase of my father and his money. Father considered the money fortunate for me—a way to get a husband. But I didn't want a husband, at least not one who took me to wife only as a bearable necessity.

Now that I knew Father had lured him in and bought him off, I couldn't really care about George. I summed George up as the same kind of man as my father, only not so shrewd. But I did care about what my father was doing to me. For years I had sat quietly in the background, doing my best to run his house and behave as he bade me. Now I stood staring at him until I drew his attention from the brandy snifter.

He started to ask if I wanted anything else, and then he saw the expression in my eyes. It stopped his question before it reached his lips, for he had never seen such an emotion—perhaps *any* emotion other than fear—in his daughter's face. It surprised him to know I could feel hatred, as it surprised me, and he was silent. I turned on my heel and left the library.

I made up my mind that I would make use of what Father represented to me, as he had made use of what I had represented to him. And so, for the next five years, I did pretty much as I pleased. I made certain that I performed my duties as mistress of Briarcliff Manor efficiently. I gave him no reason to accuse me of being a faithless daughter. There was never another George; I saw to that. There were other suitors, but none ever got so far as my father's library. Rather than give father what he sought, I preferred to remain unmarried. If he was disappointed he did not let me see it, and if he knew of the men who asked to speak to him, he never heard it from me.

He brought a series of young men to Briarcliff Manor himself, each one hopeful of being groomed to manage Father's business and properties. All of them failed for one reason or another. Finally, one stayed—I wasn't at all sure *why*, for he was not one of the chosen ones. He was the one who did all the work. Perhaps that alone is why he remained—I don't know—but Father was long past the time when he wanted personally to tend to the workmen and their problems. He wanted only to look over his private little empire, and to be assured that all was right and in good order. Darien Varka was the man to do the work and keep it in order, though I am sure Father couldn't have realized his value. If he had there would have been no need to marry me off or to bring in the others, hoping one of them would be fit to succeed him.

By the time I was twenty-four, Father had given up hope of my marrying. I was very restless, and weary of the tense and hostile life I led. The letter from Sue Ellen's mother came as a blessing. Sue Ellen had married a man named Willis, who had recently been killed in a buggy accident. Her mother feared for her health, and asked if I would be free to accompany Sue Ellen on a trip to the Continent.

I did not hesitate for a second. Even under such unhappy circumstances I looked forward to being with Sue Ellen again, and more than anything I wanted to be away from Briarcliff Manor.

As soon as Sue Ellen's period of mourning was over, we found ourselves in a whirl of balls and supper parties. The people at the parties were fun, the dances light, the dresses pretty, and I found it easy to laugh and talk to these people who did not know of my father and his money, or the bait to an empire I represented.

30

When the message came from my Father to return to Briar-cliff Manor immediately, I nearly refused to answer it. Sue Ellen suggested that I simply leave it on the table for the maid to sweep into the ashcan along with the other invitations I had refused. I found it hard to ignore her suggestion, and I did not like leaving Sue Ellen alone in Europe. But Father had demanded nothing of me in recent years, so I felt obliged to return. I believed I could leave again if I chose, and return to England if it suited me. Aside from refusing me money, he couldn't stop me, and I was reasonably certain he would not permit his daughter to roam the world penniless.

Yes, I decided, whatever he wanted must be important. I would return. Sue Ellen and I once more parted, and again I left behind a pleasant life to face what lay in store for me at Briarcliff Manor.

*3*

I ARRIVED HOME THE FIRST week of September 1867. Everything was touched by a burning autumn gold. The sun, the trees, the whole world seemed to have been gilded that day of my return.

Darien Varka came to meet me and take me to the house. I had forgotten, or had never noticed, how handsome he was. As he walked toward me, the sun glinted red in the chestnut of his hair. His voice was deep and gentle as he welcomed me home. I wondered why Father had never seen in this tall man a successor to himself. If I hadn't known that any suggestion made by me would have met with immediate disfavor, I would have spoken to Father about it.

I could hardly take my eyes from Darien. His eyes were a deep dark brown, the color I had always wished mine were. He asked me about my luggage. I had brought only part of it with me, the rest being sent by express. I indicated the three trunks to him. I looked around me, in search of someone to assist him in carrying them. Before I realized what was happening, he had picked them up as if they were jackstraws and put them into the carriage.

I hope I am wrong, but I believe my mouth was open. Darien smiled. His teeth were strikingly white against his deeply tanned skin. My trip had indeed had an effect on me, I thought. I was being very fanciful.

"How is my father?" I asked. "I was worried when I received his letter." If anything could help me regain my normal objectivity it was the subject of Father.

Darien looked over at me, smiling again. "You have no cause to worry. Your father is well, and in quite good spirits."

"Do you know why he asked me to return?"

"I do."

"Please tell me, Darien."

"I think he would prefer to tell you that himself," he said. "After all, you have crossed an entire ocean to get this far. Briarcliff Manor is only minutes farther."

I could see that he was not going to be persuaded to alleviate my curiosity, so we talked of other things.

"Do you actually manage all the Briarcliff Manor lands, Darien?"

"More or less," he said. "Of course, I consult frequently with your father, but he leaves most of the actual business in my hands." He turned toward me and grinned. "Until, of course, he finds a suitable replacement."

I had to laugh at the idea that both of us—probably everyone but Father—knew exactly who the most able manager of Briarcliff Manor would be. As Darien talked on about the estate, I realized that I knew little about it, and had never even seen all of it.

"Would you like me to show you around the rest of Briarcliff Manor?" he asked, reading my thoughts.

"Oh, yes! I would like that very much. I don't understand how I could have lived there all my life and never seen all of it."

"That wouldn't be difficult. It's large, and its boundaries are quite irregular. One point of it is at least fifteen miles from the main house."

"My word, I had no idea! No wonder Father has tried to impress upon me the extent of the estate."

He laughed, but offered no comment.

I was pleased at the proposed venture with Darien. I stole a glance at him to see if he shared my anticipation, but I could not tell. I saw only a straight profile with a strong proud chin. Again I chided myself for being full of dreams left over from too many pleasant nights abroad. I must remember that I was home again, and things were very different here.

We arrived at the front entrance to the house. Darien helped me from the carriage with all due haste and I found myself aware of the strength of the man, the touch of his hands on my waist, the fresh outdoors smell of his skin as he swept me from my seat safely to the ground.

I didn't have time to chastise myself this time, for Father appeared in the doorway. He had never greeted me before, and I was more than surprised. His face was different, too —animated, almost excited.

"I have a great surprise for you," he said. "Come with me, Annabel.

I followed—was nearly pulled, as he took hold of my wrist—and propelled me into the house.

I glanced back to throw a thank you in Darien's direction. He was standing where he had set me on firm ground, feet apart, arms folded, and grinning like a cat at my discomposed state, and the haste with which I was being towed into the house.

When I met her I'm certain my hair was askew, my hat at a rakish angle, and my face flushed. Her name was Miriam Asherton, and she would be my father's wife. I guessed her to be only a few years older than myself, and I was nearly right. She would be thirty-one on her next birthday, and I would be twenty-five on mine.

I had never thought of Father remarrying at this late date —certainly not a bride so much younger than himself—and I simply did not know how to react. She was a small woman, well rounded. Maliciously I thought that she was built well for bearing children—no doubt his reason for marrying her. But as I looked at him, I knew that if childbearing was a consideration, it was only one, for there was something decidedly different about him.

In spite of my pleasure in seeing this kind of change in my father, I was completely unable to fit Miriam into any picture I had of him. I did not know why, but I did not care for her. Her mouth was hard, and her eyes held no warmth, although she greeted me in a very demonstrative fashion.

"My dear Annabel, your father has told me so much about you, I feel that we are old friends already. I know it will be such fun shopping and getting acquainted. I have longed for the companionship of another woman."

She might have gone on forever, but Father interrupted her.

"Don't you think Annabel should meet our other guests, before you talk her to death?"

The others were two cousins of Miriam's, who had come to be part of the wedding party.

Clarissa Barington was one year younger than I, and Michael Barington was about thirty-two. The very composite of all I had envied in the girls I had known at school, Clarissa was dainty and pretty in little-girl fashion. Her face was framed with soft wisps of waving blond hair, and her eyes were the color of a cornflower touched by the sun and full of gaiety.

Even though I didn't know Michael, I was momentarily relieved in thinking this very good-looking young man to be her brother. At least, I thought, there would be no parlor games in which I would have to compete with Clarissa. Belatedly, I felt a pang as my mind shot back to Darien and the effect someone like Clarissa might have on him. In any event, my moment of relief about Michael was short-lived, for I soon discovered that Clarissa and Michael were only second cousins who had happened to come down the family line with the same last name.

When Michael took my hand firmly in his, I was still off in my own private sphere. He was dressed very fashionably, but my wayward mind immediately decided I would prefer to see him in the red jacket and black breeches of the hunt. It would suit his dark eyes and hair. He must have thought me a fool, as indeed I was. I had spent the whole day in idle imaginings about people, which was entirely unlike me. I had seen Darien as an exciting romantic figure, my father as a changed man,

Miriam as sinister and untrustworthy, Clarissa as a rival, and now Michael riding through the woods flashing red among the trees in pursuit of his quarry, with, of course, me at his side.

We were all standing in the hallway, and it rapidly became uncomfortable. Father did not seem to notice. Clarissa was becoming quite restless, as she had little else to say to any of us. I tried to look as though I welcomed Miriam's attempts at friendship.

The only one who seemed to be aware of the awkwardness of the situation was Michael. He was an interesting man to watch. He was built very compactly, as though he were used to physical labor, and yet he had a cool self-assurance that I had always associated with men of a more studious nature. His most striking feature, however, was his eyes. They were nearly black. It was difficult to see the pupil, and they had an intensity that was disconcerting. He looked from one of us to the other, seemingly aware of the increasing strain between us, but he was not a part of it at all. It was as if he were watching each of us act out our parts while he stood back comfortably enjoying the amusing aspects of an error in progress.

He had been standing by the staircase, his weight supported by his arm on the newel post. He looked at me, and suddenly I began to feel very restless too, and found myself behaving much like Clarissa, unable to keep my feet still or recall what was being said. He stood up very straight and took a step forward, bringing himself into the midst of the group, and by my side.

He said nothing for a moment. Father was reminiscing about an incident that had occurred when he and Miriam had spent a week at a friend's country home. He was apparently sure that this would inform me in no uncertain terms what a fine woman Miriam was, but I had lost the conversation some time ago, and had no idea what he was referring to. But if Michael had thought his presence would curtail Father's monologue, he was sadly mistaken. Father kept talking and gesturing at me, making sure I did not miss anything. He had not even noticed that Michael had moved into the group.

Michael finally took advantage of a split-second pause.

"Annabel, you must be very tired. Shall we all go to the parlor, where we can be more comfortable?"

He turned his attention from me to the others. Clarissa's face lit up, and she began to walk toward the parlor before anyone had answered.

Michael escorted me into the parlor. I had never really cared for this room. It had a heavy look and lacked the grace, or perhaps the character, that it should have had. The furniture had simply been placed and left where it was. It was a large square room, and could easily have been given to a cozy seating arrangement. Instead, Father's hand had touched it, and small groups of chairs were set in isolated corners so that we were forced either to crowd together in one of the corners or be spread all over, preventing any conversation. Michael scanned the room quickly as we entered, and took me to the two sofas that faced one another by the fireplace. It would be crowded, but it was the only place that all of us could sit together.

We all squeezed into our places. Again Michael seemed to drift away from us. He went across the room and brought another chair to the group, which he used. I did not recall ever having met anyone who behaved that way.

I managed to stumble through a half hour of conversation with the four of them before begging off. I had not yet managed to say a single sensible thing, and was very self-conscious. I was continuously blushing, which was not only out of character for me but very annoying. I thought I must be tired, and would certainly be more myself when I returned for tea.

I rose from my seat and made my excuses—very well, I thought. As I edged my way from between the sofa and the low table in front of it, I tripped. Michael quickly caught me, supporting my arm as I disengaged my foot from the hem of Clarissa's gown. He was admirably kind, his expression serious and understanding, and that did much to ease my embarrassment as I extricated myself and apologized to Clarissa. It was not until I was again free that I saw that the sympathetic expression on Michael's face did not match the merriment in his eyes. Before I could do anything else unseemingly, I hastened from the parlor, mortified by the impression I had made on Father's guests.

I went upstairs to my rooms. Darien had seen to it that my luggage was brought up, and Lettie was busy unpacking for me. I was tempted to tell her to leave and finish later, but I knew there were many things I would be wanting and it was best to be done with the task now. I went to my sitting room and shut both the door to the hall and the one to the bedroom. Somehow I had to get hold of myself, and I needed to be alone to do so.

Each of my feelings seemed so strong and in such contrast to the others that I did not know what to make of them. I had disliked Miriam instinctively, and had made such a fool of myself afterward, that it was difficult to trust any of my first impressions. I hoped what I was feeling was a natural reaction to the fatigue of traveling and the shock of Father's unexpected announcement. I sat back in a comfortable chair near the window, letting the tension fall away from me as I waited for Lettie to finish my room. I thought I might give anything to slip into a warm, refreshing bath.

I was gazing out across the lush green lawn that narrowed into a channel bordered by huge hemlocks. The dazzling sun made it shimmer with color. The breeze had dropped to nothing, and the scene was motionless until a horse and rider came into view from the direction of the stables. At first, thinking the others had remained in the parlor, I did not know who it was, but soon I realized it was Miriam. Though she broke the calm stillness of the scene, she was a pretty addition to it. The pale-lavender sash of her riding hat flowed out behind her as her horse sped toward the hemlock woods.

I sat watching her progress, paying little attention, merely enjoying the scene. I don't know how long the other rider had been at the edge of the woods, for I did not notice him until Miriam had nearly reached him. At first I thought it was my father, but the hair was too dark. Michael? I didn't think so. Michael had appeared earlier in very neat fashionable clothes, and this man appeared to be wearing ordinary work clothes. And it did not seem reasonable that Michael would remain under the protection of the hemlocks. He could certainly go riding with his cousin whenever he wished. He had no need to be secretive.

Lettie came out of my room.

"Your clothes are laid in place, miss." I thanked her and we chatted for a moment.

"Can you bring me some bath water now, Lettie?"

"Yes, miss." She left to do as I bade. When I looked back to the edge of the lawn, both riders had disappeared. Tiredness was taking the edge off my curiosity, and the promise of a bath and clean clothes dismissed the matter from my mind.

When I went down to tea, I felt much fresher. I put on one of the gowns I had bought in France and, when I had satisfied myself as to my appearance, went directly to the East Terrace. We had always served tea there when the weather permitted. It was one of my favorite spots, for it gave a beautiful view of the lawn I had just been watching from upstairs in my room. When I came on the terrace, I thought it strange that there was no activity or preparation, but I supposed that tea would be late today. I sat for nearly twenty minutes without seeing anyone. Finally I grew restless and wondered if some accident had occurred. I went to the kitchen. All seemed normal; in fact the help were all sitting about the kitchen table having their own tea.

Lettie saw me first, and jumped to her feet.

"Yes, miss? Is there something you wish?"

Jacobs, now on his feet, added, "We did not hear you ring, miss."

I hope I did not look as puzzled as I felt. "I was wondering when tea would be served, Jacobs. And, Jacobs, why have you served yourselves tea before you have served us?"

"But, miss . . ." He stammered, losing all of his customary mannerisms. "Tea was served some twenty minutes ago."

"It has? But I was just on the terrace. There was no tea."

He looked embarrassed, and his voice was apologetic.

"The East Terrace, miss?"

"Of course, the East Terrace!"

40

"I am sorry, miss, I thought that you would have been told. We now serve tea on the front terrace. Miss Asherton prefers it there."

I held my head a little higher, feeling very much the fool. Why had no one seen fit to inform me of this change in routine? I could see that adjusting to Miriam's rule of the house would not be easy. It was one aspect of my father's marriage I had not considered.

Besides making a spectacle of myself in front of the servants, I would now be compelled to walk into tea quite late, and needing to explain myself. I felt Miriam's actions high-handed and thoughtless. My feelings toward my father were no softer. He had not informed me of the new tea location—nor of my sudden change in status. I felt he owed me at least the courtesy of letting me know that I was no longer in charge of the household. Of course, I would have expected it after the wedding, but I had not dreamed Miriam would be the ruling hand already.

Reluctantly, I headed for the North Terrace. They were all gathered in a compact group, happily chatting about the coming wedding. For a moment I thought I might slip in unnoticed, but Michael caught sight of me. Immediately he was on his feet, taking me by the arm to his chair, which he gave to me. It was then I noticed that it was the only empty chair. Miriam had not only failed to inform me of the change, but she had not intended that I discover it for myself. Her attitude seemed most peculiar in view of her exceedingly warm welcome earlier, and I wondered what purpose she might have.

She looked up as Michael seated me. There was no sign in her face that anything was amiss. She greeted me in that cheerful voice which did not carry to her eyes or the expression of her mouth.

"I didn't expect to have the pleasure of seeing you for tea, dear. We thought you would be too tired to come down. I should have known better." She tittered and looked over at my father. "John has told me what a traveler you are."

She placed her hand over her breast in an exaggerated

gesture, rolling her eyes up as she said, "Oh, how I do envy you. It must be nice to travel so easily. It always tires me terribly."

She chatted on about the woes of traveling. I paid little attention to what she was saying until I heard, "Even the trip to and from the guest house is a trial. John, dear, don't you believe we could all come over here to the main house now that Annabel is home again?" She laughed, looking coyly from my father to myself. "She should make an adequate chaperone, don't you think?"

Miriam turned her gaze fully on my father, her prominent eyes waiting expectantly for an affirmative reply. Father did not answer immediately, and for that moment my heart fluttered with the hope that he was going to refuse. But he smiled and agreed. I felt disappointed.

I had to get control of myself. I had a deep aversion to this woman, and for reasons that had no foundation I did not want her in this house. I didn't need to remind myself how ridiculous this was; a man would naturally bring his bride to his home, and after all, in a matter of a week she would be his wife. Unexpectedly, my mind went back to earlier this afternoon, and again I wondered whom she had met in the woods and why.

Miriam was delighted with her new state of affairs, but did not seem the least surprised at it. Michael said little throughout tea, and as he had remained standing behind my chair, I could not see the expression on his face. Clarissa acted as though nothing had been said, and continued busily to consume another chocolate éclair. How she could eat as she did and keep her trim figure, I did not know.

I have always enjoyed tea, but today I was heartily glad to escape the company of our houseguests. Miriam went in search of Darien to help her move her luggage to the main house. I was startled when she said she would be back and unpacked in time for dinner at eight. I considered such a fast move quite a feat for one who claimed to be undone by the mere ride between the two houses, but I did not waste my breath in voicing my opinion.

42

Not wanting to return to my room, I left the terrace by the front steps and went toward the East Lawn. I had no more than turned the corner of the house when I saw Darien talking with the head gardener. His stance was relaxed. It was a relief to see someone speaking with honest animation in his face. Darien, at least, was not afraid to let a person see what he was thinking.

As I walked, trying to shake my troubling thoughts, something niggled at the back of my mind. I believe it came to me as Darien turned and caught sight of me. It was the turn of his head, or perhaps the angle of the sun, but I knew in that moment that it was he whom Miriam had ridden to meet earlier. My heart sank. My feelings were completely out of proportion to what I knew of Darien, but I most ardently wished he were as I had thought, open and free in mind. If he turned out to be otherwise, then he would indeed be the worst of the lot, for it would mean he had a great ability to disguise his feelings.

He walked toward me with loose-jointed grace, smiling. The look of him served only to heighten the feeling of apprehension which was rapidly taking hold of me. All the ease of our earlier conversation disappeared, and I sounded like a tongue-tied schoolgirl. He cocked his head to one side, looking intently at me, then took me by the arm and led me to a bench closeted by an array of dogwood trees and azaleas.

"What has happened to you since this afternoon?" he asked.

I shook my head to indicate nothing—nothing that I could talk to him about. His finger lifted my chin so my eyes met the deep reddish brown of his own. I found it difficult to think that eyes such as his could be hiding deceit.

"Didn't you get on with Miriam?"

"Miriam!" I said too loudly. He grinned, looking slightly ashamed at being caught in this impropriety.

"Well . . . Mrs. Asherton."

"Why did you call her Miriam?"

"She asked me to," he said with annoying simplicity.

Common sense as well as courtesy dictated that I should tell him immediately that she was at this moment searching for him, but I didn't. It might have been that I didn't want her to move in that evening, but I also wanted to talk to Darien, hoping he would give me some assurance that he was not involved with her.

"Did you just say *Mrs*. Asherton?" I asked.

"Yes. After you reminded me I must when talking to . . . certain members of the family." His eyes were alight with deviltry, but I paid him no heed.

"I didn't know she was a widow. She seems very young for that, and I thought I understood Jacobs to call her Miss Asherton."

He smiled.

"I suppose she *is* young, but Mrs. Asherton has managed to be widowed twice in her life."

"Oh, I am sorry. That is too bad; it must have been very difficult for her."

Darien was quiet for a moment, and seemed to be considering something. Finally he said, "I can assure you it was too bad, and it did cause her some very bad moments."

I wanted to ask more, but I no longer knew how. Most of all I wanted to know how he knew so much about her, but I had begun to feel wary, and I didn't want him to realize it.

"Mrs. Asherton is looking for you now," I said, as I should have at the very outset.

The words did not fit the trend of our conversation, and in great measure restored some of the easiness of our earlier talk. He was again gently teasing me.

"I see. And do you know what she wants of me?"

My chin went up.

"Yes, I do. She wished you to move her luggage up to the main house. I believe she is hopeful of accomplishing this yet today."

He began to laugh. His eyes never left my face, and with regret I saw that he fully realized I had detained him deliberately. He raised his eyebrows and still smiling, drawled, "And was she in a hurry to locate me?"

I found it difficult to speak without laughing. "I believe she might have been."

44

He said nothing else, but bowed and left me to go toward the house. I didn't move from my seat. My mind was a whirl of misgivings and embarrassment over my peculiar behavior with Darien.

The dogwood grove was one of my favorite hideaways at Briarcliff Manor, and I had often come there as a child. It was possible to peek between the branches and see the house, and the path that led to the stables, but I didn't think anyone could see in. It had served for years as my playhouse, later as a haven to sort out the troubles of growing up. Now it sheltered me from I knew not what.

As I looked up, I saw Michael and Clarissa walking leisurely across the lawn toward the dogwoods. Michael looked in my direction just as I peeked out at them. I felt myself physically pulling back. I was certain he had seen me. I did not want to see anyone, and I was in no mood to listen to Clarissa talk her nonsense. I edged forward on my seat, cautiously peeking between the branches of the trees. Michael was still looking directly at me, and Clarissa had not paused in her talking or gesturing. I was about to give up hope when he placed his hand on her arm, guiding her away from my haven. Clarissa beamed up at him, her eyes twinkling.

I could not be sure whether Michael had left me in peace out of kindness or because he had not actually seen me, but I left immediately to go to my room before he had a chance to change his mind. It seemed to be the only safe spot for me. I closed the draperies against the last rays of the dying sun and sank into a chair. My head ached, and I couldn't remember when I had felt so tired or so old.

I must have sat in the growing dusk for a full hour before I began to dress for dinner. I wished only to put on one of my old, dull dresses, to look as nondescript and unnoticeable as possible. I knew I couldn't. It may have been pride, awakened by Miss Hamilton and Sue Ellen, or it may have been stubbornness, but I did not want Miriam or any of the others to realize what an effect they had on me. I might have been displaced, made to seem a guest in my own home, but at least I could keep these feelings to myself.

I dressed with great care. I took my hair down and brushed it until it gleamed like highly polished mahogany in the wavering light from my candle. I carefully formed each coil of hair atop my head, making certain it was smooth and neatly in place. The dress I had chosen was of a Nile-green silk trimmed lightly with cording of a slightly darker shade. It was rather severely tailored for the evening, but it became me, and I felt satisfied. I had decided to make a striking appearance—and to learn all I could about these people who now considered my home their own.

# 4

Now that my decision had been made, and I was dressed to my satisfaction, I felt more comfortable. I descended the stairs, listening carefully as I went for the sounds of voices. I did not want to make the mistake again of going to a room we customarily used, only to find that Miriam had changed the custom in my absence. I heard laughter coming from the right. That would mean the library, the morning room, or the front parlor. I crossed the main hall and went toward the library, the most likely of the three rooms, for it was by far the coziest.

A cheering fire against the chilly autumn night crackled and danced, making the room leap with tongues of color. As I entered, Clarissa was twirling prettily, showing off to good advantage a new salmon-colored gown. The firelight gave her face a look of warmth that in another woman might have been lit from within. She glanced through long lashes at each of the admiring gentlemen in the room. The cut of her dress and the radiance of her face made me feel quite spinsterish in my own gown. I was still standing in the doorway, my eyes sweeping the scene, when Darien took notice of me.

As he rose, his gaze only for me, Michael too noticed my entrance. Either I had made a faux pas or was enticing them as had Clarissa, for everyone in the room looked in my direction.

I drew myself up as though I were approaching a great ordeal. Darien took me into the room. In my heart I thanked him, wondering if he could possibly know in what manner he had rescued me from my doubts and misgivings.

The others settled into their seats, not half as happily, I noted, as before. Michael's face had the look of a thundercloud, and Miriam had no kind look for anyone. I glanced in her direction and was puzzled, for I could see she was displeased with Michael. Strangest of all, she did not seem to want me with Darien. I was very confused, and did not see why my presence seemed to cause her so much consternation. I did not know what she had in mind, but if she did not wish me to be with Darien, I would do my best to see that he remained my escort for the evening.

And since no one had bothered to tell me I was no longer mistress of Briarcliff Manor, I could hardly be expected to act otherwise. With Darien's strong arm to give me courage, I took a deep breath and greeted my father, and for the first time addressed and greeted each of the others as though they were my guests. It did wonders for me, and the expressions on the faces around the room were a kaleidoscope of shock and surprise, except for Michael and Darien. Each of them seemed to be enjoying his own private joke.

Whatever had pulled Michael out of his momentary gloom, I was glad of it. I returned my attention to my father, who was sputtering and mumbling from the depths of the red leather chair by the fire. I am now certain the man was as puzzled at the change my trip had made in me as I was at the changes in the house. He looked rapidly from Miriam to me, his eyes finally resting on me as I watched the familiar look of disdain creep over his features.

"Sit down, Annabel . . . over there."

He exhaled a deep breath of air through his nose as he indicated a straight-backed chair, well away from the others. It was so like father to make his point with dramatics.

"Thank you, no, Father. I prefer this one," I said as I seated myself in a deep-violet chair which complemented the color of my gown.

"Michael," I said sweetly, "would you please bring me a small glass of sherry."

"You won't have time for that," said my father. "Dinner will be served at any moment."

"I am afraid that is so, Annabel," added Miriam. "We didn't know when you might be down, after this afternoon's late tea . . . well, we just weren't sure, so we planned to go ahead."

I said nothing to them, but waited patiently for my sherry. I wished I had not asked it of Michael. After his mercurial change of moods just moments ago, I did not know if I could count on him. I stole one look at him to verify I wanted the sherry, and then inclined my head, hoping that he would feel unable to refuse me. I needn't have worried, for Michael was all grace and charm, and my sherry was in my hand in short order.

Miriam was another matter. She rang the small bell on the table beside her, and Jacobs entered immediately. He looked first to her, and then to me. It was a certainty that the servants had been discussing the new state of affairs. Two mistresses in one house was not an easy situation for anyone. I stood up so as to gain his full attention.

"Jacobs! Please serve dinner in fifteen minutes," I said.

"Yes, miss."

Again he turned to Miriam as he bowed and left the room. Much to my delight, Miriam looked for all the world like a goldfish who had landed outside her bowl. Her mouth was working soundlessly, and her eyes, naturally prominent, were bulging. I was so close to bursting into laughter that I took a large sip of sherry, which caused me to choke but at least stopped the impulse to laugh.

The fifteen-minute delay I had asked of Jacobs seemed to last an eternity. Suddenly no one had much to say. Michael, now seemingly in a permanent good humor, made a gallant attempt to make the weather an interesting subject. He found little cooperation until he began to speak of the gardens and the grounds of Briarcliff Manor. Darien then joined in. One had only to look at Darien's face to see that this was a subject of which he would not tire. The rest of us listened with interest as his words formed a picture of Briarcliff Manor that was different in its beauty and meaning from any I had ever heard. Even my father seemed fascinated, and he paid close attention to all that was said.

Finally Jacobs opened the library doors and announced dinner. Darien was by my side before anyone else had a chance to rise. A feeling of warmth flowed through me. Tonight I was not going to let any apprehension spoil my evening. As if Darien had read my thoughts, he led me from the room ahead of the others and took me to the seat at the foot of the table. Nothing could go wrong this evening! My father shot a furious glance in my direction as he brought Miriam into the room. She looked down at the seat by which I was standing, then moved slowly to the chair adjacent to father's. A seat for a guest. I knew Father was furious, but I was also certain that he would do nothing in front of the others.

We all sat down looking very proper, Clarissa and Michael on one side of the table, and Miriam and Darien on the other. This was the first time I had ever known Darien to eat with us—another of Miriam's innovations, I learned later, and the only one for which I heartily thanked her. Having told my father an evening should be composed of couples if at all possible, she had arranged for Darien to be Clarissa's escort and Michael to be mine. I could then understand her displeasure in the way we had paired off that night. It was only what she deserved, for by now it was obvious that Michael held Clarissa's attention, and I assumed the feeling was returned—or, at least, not turned in my direction.

These little discoveries raised my spirits more than I could say, and served to give me a feeling of invincibility as far as Miriam was concerned. She obviously didn't know people well. I smiled to myself and saw with satisfaction, as I turned my attention back to Darien, that Clarissa was happily entertaining Michael with her chatter.

Miriam sat through the entire dinner looking pleasant and acting the perfect guest. I had to admire her composure. She was attentive to my father, flashing her smile at him, including him in everything she said.

"John and I were so pleased you were able to return in time for the wedding. We were worried that you might be between stops and out of reach of our message. But everything is turning out perfectly, just as John said it would." She beamed at my father and then continued. "I suppose you will want to be off again as soon as possible after the wedding is over."

She had nearly spoken the thoughts I had had earlier. I did not want to remain at Briarcliff Manor; I wished to return to a happier way of life. But as I heard her speak the words, my earlier, irrational dislike came upon me, and I was not certain I should leave, not until I had satisfied myself that nothing was amiss. I tried to look surprised as I answered her.

"Whatever has given you the idea I wish to travel again so soon? I really had not thought to be off again. There will be much to be done around the Manor, and—"

"But, my dear!" Miriam cut in. "You mustn't let your father or me change your plans. We certainly wouldn't want to interfere with your life."

I felt she was saying a good deal more than her words indicated.

"Don't worry, Miriam," I said, a little more sharply than I had intended. "You won't be interfering in my life. I shall travel again, when I choose to."

My father looked up at me.

"Annabel! There is no need to be rude. Miriam is trying to be patient with you, but your attitude is far from receptive."

Miriam looked as though she had just been canonized.

"I am sorry, Father, I didn't realize Miriam's feelings were so delicate." I daintily patted my mouth with my napkin. "You know I've always spoken my mind."

I wondered if he would make any comment to that, for I had never in my life spoken my mind, at least not to him. But he showed no reaction, so I turned to Miriam.

"Please forgive me if I have upset you."

I fervently hoped she caught the look in my eye as I spoke. By this time I was certain she had a hide as thick as a rhinoceros and would not, could not, be offended by anything I might say or do.

We finished the last few bites of a delicious torte, and then rose to adjourn to the small front parlor. The men were anxious to get to the smoking room and their brandies.

Clarissa had taken possession of Michael's arm as we left the dining room; following her lead, I did the same to Darien. He alone had made it a pleasant homecoming day for me. We stood in a cluster finishing the last bits of conversations begun at the dinner table.

I kept looking at Clarissa and Michael. Clarissa's actions were obvious enough, but I could not read Michael at all. He was kind and attentive to her, but he had behaved like that to everyone, including me. Nor could I understand Miriam. Why would she try to bring me between Michael and Clarissa if they were interested in one another? I would have thought she would be pleased for them. And it seemed to make no sense that she had tried to persuade me to leave Briarcliff Manor and, at the same time, involve me with a man living there.

We broke into segregated little groups, ladies to the parlor, and gentlemen off to smoke and talk of things they considered too rough or too important for our ears.

Miriam, Clarissa, and I had little to say to one another, so Miriam and I ended by listening to Clarissa dreamily talk of men. Her chatter did nothing to aid me in sorting out these people and the characteristics I felt it necessary to know of them. Clarissa was interested in all men. Apparently she was an inveterate flirt, and simply chose to give her undivided attention to whatever man she deemed most handsome or attractive at the moment. Miriam sat with an air of tried patience. Clarissa's opinions did not seem new to her. The men returned, and we made a few feeble attempts at making the remainder of the evening pleasant.

There was little for it. We were not a cohesive group, so the evening ended early. Darien left at the earliest opportunity, and I had never been more pleased to seek the comfort of my room.

As cheerfully as possible I bade everyone a good night and escaped up the stairs. The bed had been turned down, and it looked fresh and inviting. I undressed quickly and got into bed.

The only light in the room was a small candle on my nightstand that flickered, casting wavering shadows on the walls. I blew it out and snuggled into the quilt to wait for quiet to overtake the rest of the house. Again aware of how much better the others seemed to get along without my presence, I heard them milling about in the hallway. An occasional laugh broke out, and then one by one the bedroom doors closed.

I must have fallen asleep immediately, for I woke very early the next morning. The sun was just coming up, and it reminded me of the many mornings I had awakened early as a young girl, anxious for the first rays of the morning sun. We had Jules at that time, the kind old groom who'd taught me how to ride early in the mornings. My father had never given permission for me to be taught. As with most things concerning me, he put off my desire for another day. The day never came, so Jules taught me at dawn, before anyone else had begun to stir. Stealthily we would walk the horses out across the East Lawn, through the hemlock woods to a clearing. There he would instruct me. I had loved Jules with all my heart, and I think he loved me as my father never could.

Jules had long since died, but I had Bucephalus, the horse he had chosen for me the day after my father finally admitted that I knew how to ride.

That was a day I shall not readily forget. The sun was hidden by cold misty clouds, and I could barely bestir myself. Shivering and shaking, I had dressed, putting on an extra coat. I tiptoed past Father's door and, as usual, heard nothing. Many times I had wished he snored, so I could be certain he was in his room asleep. I continued on and hurried to the door of the kitchen where Jules met me each morning. He was there, but I had no need to open the door to know something was amiss.

I was about to turn and run like a rabbit back to the safety of my bed when the door opened from the outside, slamming against the wall.

"Where are you going, young lady?"

I stopped in my tracks, but hadn't the courage to turn and face my father. His big hand came down upon my shoulder and spun me around.

"I'm sorry, little missy," said Jules. "I shouldn't have encouraged you."

"Quiet!" my father shouted. "Why have you been sneaking about the grounds, Annabel?"

"I wanted to ride a horse, Father."

"And when you can not get your way by request, you will sneak about doing as you please behind my back. Is that right, Annabel?"

"No! I'm not a sneak. I just wanted to learn how to ride a horse. You said I could someday."

He stalked out of the house, taking me by the arm. I had to run to keep up with him. He was hurting my wrist, but I didn't say anything.

"Which horse is it she rides?" he asked Jules.

Robbie was standing all saddled and ready for me. Jules brought him to my father.

"Let me see you ride," he said.

I mounted—and, though I did not do as well as usual, Robbie did the work for me.

I was just beginning to enjoy myself when I heard Father call out, "Dismount!" I did as he said immediately, and walked back to where he stood.

"You like these morning trysts of yours?"

"Yes, Father. Very much. Did you see how well Jules has taught me?"

"You ride well enough, but I see he encouraged you to creep about behind my back, and I won't stand for that, Annabel. Not from a servant, and especially not from my daughter."

"But, Father! I want to ride—*can't* I ride Robbie?"

"Ladies ride in the afternoon. Escorted."

I was certain then that I should never ride again. Who would escort me? I simply could not picture Aggie on a horse, and there was no one else. I went home with Father, defeated.

The following afternoon, Aggie came to my room.

"It's time for your afternoon ride, Miss Annabel," she said, laying my riding habit on the bed. I asked no questions, but dressed as quickly as possible.

54

Jules was standing out in front of the house. He had his horse, and in his right hand he held the reins of the most beautiful horse I had ever seen.

"He is yours, Miss Annabel. His name is Bucephalus."

"Mine? Is he really mine?"

Jules had tears in his eyes, but I had stars in mine.

"Did you give him to me, Jules? How *could* you?"

"No, miss, I picked him, but it's your father what give him to you."

"Father? Father is giving me a horse?"

"Aw, miss, he is proud of you, and isn't knowing how to say it."

"Oh, Jules! I don't know what to say—he's *beautiful!* This is the best day of my life."

And it had been. For a moment, through the eyes of Jules, I had seen my father care for me, though it would never come from *his* lips. Father never mentioned the gift of Bucephalus, never asked if I was pleased.

Nor did I ever find a moment in which I felt I might thank him.

Now, still thinking of my father, Jules, and the present groom, Matthew, I rose quickly and put on my riding habit. Checking myself in the mirror, I adjusted my hat and ran my hands down the slim lines of my waist. I might never be the girlish young thing that Clarissa was, but I was pleased to note that I had learned to dress to take advantage of the qualities I did have. Even my eyes could be made to show well with the right colors. I turned again, slowly, enjoying the look of myself.

When I got there Matthew was in the stables, although he looked but half awake. I had to smile, wondering which of the servant girls had kept him from his sleep last night.

"Good morning, miss. It's good to have you back." He grinned up at me through sleepy eyes. "You be wanting an early ride?"

"Yes, please, Matthew."

He walked into the stables, passing by Bucephalus' stall.

"Matthew—I want to ride *my* horse."

He hesitated, and I thought he was going to say something

to me, but he went about his work and soon brought Bucephalus to me.

"You won't be riding alone, will you, miss?"

"Yes, I will, Matthew. But don't worry, I'm not going far."

He *did* look worried, and he momentarily reminded me of a younger version of Jules. Jules, more careful of me than my father had ever been, had never let me venture out alone. Jules was a foreigner; I suppose that explained it, for he was the only person who ever thought I was beautiful. He had never cared for my father, and he took my side in all matters. I think it was Jules who made my childhood bearable; he made me feel happy and free. Certainly at school, when the other girls would tell stories about outings with their fathers, I would describe adventures with Jules.

Now Matthew seemed to be taking over Jules's concern for me. It gave me a feeling of security and pleasure I could not describe. I assured him once more that I would be safe for a short ride.

"You stay away from the south fields, miss. That old guesthouse of Mr. Arbriar's is crumbling. It's not safe over there."

"I'm not going to the south fields," I said. "And I don't even know where the old house is. I'll just take a short ride out toward the hemlocks. It is open and smooth there."

Still shaking his head and looking worried, he let me have my leave.

I mounted and turned the horse toward the East Lawn. I had just started toward the hemlocks when I remembered Darien's promise to show me all Briarcliff Manor. I wondered when he would keep that promise, or *if* he would. This morning I didn't care. The air was clear and brisk, and the autumn colors peeking between the heavy boughs of the hemlocks were beautiful.

I returned to the house at about seven thirty. There was much bustle in the kitchen as breakfast was being readied, but no one else seemed to be about, much to my relief. I started toward the morning room, thinking to go through there on my way to the greenhouse. I liked flowers on the table, and had missed them since my return. Apparently Miriam did not share my love of their brightness.

As I passed the library on my way down the hall, I heard voices coming from the slightly open door. Though soft, they were not friendly. Feeling no hesitation whatever, I stopped and listened.

Miriam's was the first voice I recognized. She was speaking my name. I moved closer to the door, straining to hear.

"You've been no help whatsoever!" she was saying. "I must be able to depend on you, or I shall have to change my plans. She is not *at all* what John led me to expect."

"She managed to handle *you* rather well yesterday." And I recognized the cool tones of Michael's voice.

"Yes—didn't she, though! With you sitting there doing nothing, enjoying it like one of your sad jokes!"

"Come now, Miriam, you are well able to take care of yourself. You didn't really think she would sit back forever taking those nasty little barbs you tossed at her, did you?"

"That is not the point. If you had done your part, I would not have had to resort to such direct language."

Michael's voice was languid as he answered her, and the contrast between the two of them sent shivers up my spine.

"You can fight your own battles . . . or call upon your husband-to-be. Cry to *him*."

She let out a sound that was almost a growl.

"Stop it, Michael! You know John can't help me in this."

Michael's hand came down hard against something I supposed to be the desk. His voice was low and rasping with anger, and I could imagine the fury flashing in his black eyes.

"What," he snapped, "do you expect me to do? Bodily place her on a train, or perhaps kidnap her from her bed? God knows I'd take her from here if I could. Why did you send for her if you wanted her out of here?"

Miriam's voice matched his for deep anger, but it had a sharp strident tone to it.

"I didn't send for her by choice. *You* know that! John insisted. He wouldn't consider it any other way, God only knows why. They never did get along, and now here you are playing the fool for me. I am plagued by stupid mulish men."

"It must be the one sorrow of your life," Michael retorted.

"Don't continue to be foolish with me, Michael. It won't work. I know you too well. Charm her. Or is it that she is immune to your notable charm?"

Her voice had turned to acid as she mocked him. I did not want to hear his reply. Charm me? Get me to leave my own home? My experience with George and my father had made me wary of the attentions of men, but had never prepared me to deal with the deliberate maneuverings of a pair such as these. I felt sick to my stomach. They spoke as though I were a puppet, an object to be used and manipulated for their convenience. In this house there would be no respect or concern for me; my father had seen to that years ago. His own attitudes transferred easily to the others.

As I was moving away, Miriam said, "John doesn't want her here after the wedding. I don't think he ever really wanted her to come back at all. He has some idea of proving something to her, Lord knows what that might be, or why he would bother, but in any case John should cause you no worry."

I paused long enough to hear Michael's reply.

"What makes you think anything worries me? Don't keep at me, Miriam. I don't want any part in your games."

"But you agreed—"

"I am here to watch you, not to aid you, my much-widowed *cousin.*"

"Don't you threaten me, Michael!" she answered, raising her voice.

"Hush, you fool—you'll be heard!"

Michael moved toward the door. I hurried away at the sound of his footsteps and just managed to slip into the morning room as the library door opened, spilling the light from the window across the dark hallway. I stood very still, waiting to be certain they had not seen me.

The library door shut, making a definite little sound. I let my breath out and slumped against it in relief, leaning against the cool wood. How I wished I had not answered Father's request to come home. Aside from the fact that I now knew Father hadn't really wanted me, I also knew for certain that Miriam was up to something. All of them were involved, even Darien, but I could make no sense of it.

I stood for several minutes, my head pressed against the door, trying to regain my composure and untangle the confusion of purposes I had found. A hand came down gently on my shoulder; I whirled about as though I had been struck. The terrace door stood open, and I stood face to face with Michael. His look was somber, his thick black hair and his deep-set eyes gave him a forbidding look. I pulled back against the door. His hand had dropped from my shoulder, and he made no attempt to touch me again.

"You heard, didn't you?"

His voice was low, and I could not control the shiver that ran through me. I did not answer, but I tried to nod.

"Things aren't always what they seem," he said.

There was nothing I could think of to say, even if I had been able to speak. He said no more. The look on his face changed, and he pulled me toward him. My face brushed against the coarse tweed of his coat. I stiffened and pulled away from him. He had no right to treat me so familiarly. I stood erect, determined to keep my chin firm.

"I am not one to be charmed or led about by you, sir!"

If he had not been standing so close and directly in front of me, I would have made a haughty exit. As it was, I had to stand there and watch my comment register on his face. I had expected him to laugh at me, or to be affronted, or even angry, but he looked disappointed, even hurt, throwing my mind into a mixture of confusion and misery.

I no longer wanted to leave. This man was a mystery to me. He seemed to be on all sides at once. I wanted him to talk to me, make some sense out of things for me, give me the chance to apologize for my remark. But he backed away from me.

"I see. You are a very frank young woman, Miss Arbriar."

He left the room then, his dark head held proudly, a tall man with massive shoulders who moved swiftly and with athletic grace through the terrace door and out into the sun. He looked back at me, unsmiling, and went toward the stables.

He did not come to breakfast. Everyone was talking of the plans for the day. Clarissa was to spend the entire morning with the dressmaker. Miriam had to go into the city to check on some difficulties that had arisen with regard to her previous husband's will. Father was to escort her to the lawyer's and, I assumed, offer his advice. Darien, of course, had his normal duties. I alone had nothing planned for myself, and it seemed no one else had need of my company or assistance. Miriam looked up at me between bites of toast.

"What will you do today, Annabel?"

"I may go visit some friends."

She laughed a small satisfied laugh. "Oh, my, I do see why you like to travel. What friends could you possibly have way out here in the country?" She laughed again. "It must be deadly for a young girl like you."

Her eyes appraised me, denying the sincerity of her words. "You must long for dances and parties . . . and young men who are interested in you. After all, you should be concerned for your future. No one would blame you for going elsewhere."

I was certain she would not blame me; no doubt she would pack my bags for me if I gave her the chance. She would be delighted to see me leave right after the wedding, whatever her reason.

I marveled at the cool audacity of her continued prodding, but I replied as sternly as I could.

"I'm sure no one would blame me, Miriam, but you are mistaken. I enjoy the country, and I do find the few people who do live nearby friendly and interesting."

Clarissa let out a great sigh.

'I wish you would introduce them to me. I find it very quiet, and no excitement whatever."

She stretched like a kitten, her eyes turned toward Darien in Michael's absence. I ignored her antics.

"I don't think my friends could give you the kind of excitement you wish, unless, of course, you like to ride. They are very keen on that."

I waited for her to make a comment. When she did not, I asked her, *"Do* you like to ride?"

Clarissa barely looked at me, but made a face, crinkling her pert little nose.

"Not really. I prefer other things." She had lost all interest in the conversation and, having gotten no response from Darien, excused herself from the table.

Father, too, rose to excuse himself.

"Darien, I'd like to see you about the farm accounts before I leave for the city."

Darien took the last swallow from his coffee cup. "I can come with you this morning," he replied. "In the library?"

"Yes," said my father.

"All right, sir. I'll be there in twenty minutes. I'll just go by the office and get the books."

Darien hurried to his office, which was on the far side of Briarcliff near the south field. My father gave a brief nod and left the room, leaving me alone with my coffee and my thoughts.

# 5

I WONDERED IF MY BEHAVIOR had been the cause of Michael's absence from breakfast this morning. I hoped not, but I did not know what I could do about it.

I rose and went to the kitchen to check the state of our supplies, and saw at once that my worry had been for naught. Michael was sitting at the big scarred kitchen table in the midst of a rollicking flirtation with Aggie, whose cheeks were as shiny as rosy round apples. The old woman lifted her heft around with surprising agility as she giggled and served Michael breakfast. He looked so relaxed and happy that I could not believe he was the same man I had encountered earlier.

Aggie caught sight of me standing in the doorway. Her hands flew to her flaming cheeks.

"Oh, miss! I didn't see you." She tittered and looked quickly at the recalcitrant Michael. "This one has been teasing the very life from these old bones. He is a caution."

The pleasure at his teasing was still written all over her face.

"What will you be wanting, miss?"

I smiled at her and included Michael in the smile, hoping in some measure that it would serve as an apology for my previous actions.

"I came to check on the supplies, Aggie."

"Oh, no need. Mrs. Asherton has taken care of all that. The larder is well stocked."

"And the wine cellar?"

"That too, miss."

"Well, then, Aggie, I see I am to have a day of rest and leisure before me."

"It'll do you good, miss."

"I agree!" added Michael, as he came across to where we stood. "For now she can give me some of her free time."

Aggie had begun to act giddy again, and her face had broken into a smile as soon as he came near her. He pinched her cheek and winked at her. He seemed irrepressible when in such a mood, and I felt pulled in two directions. Part of me wanted to join the fun, and part of me shrank from the complete freedom of his actions. He took me by the arm, cutting short any reply I might have made.

For someone I had thought to have been offended so recently, he was certainly in high spirits. He whisked me out of the kitchen door. My hand flew to my hatless head as we came into the brilliant sunlight.

"What's the matter?" He grinned down at me. "Afraid you'll spoil that beautiful complexion?"

"Yes!" I lied.

He leaned back through the door and grabbed a garden hat from the hook inside the door. He mashed it on my head, causing my hair to droop miserably across my right eye. I let out a huff of air and drew myself up to full height.

He burst out laughing; I had never heard a man laugh with such complete abandon. I was forced to join him, knowing full well what a spectacle I must look. He stopped suddenly, and his face grew soft.

"You are so beautiful when you are happy."

My laughter died in my throat. No one had ever spoken to me like that before. A deep warm feeling flowed through me. His hand reached out; he waited for me to place mine into it. As much as I wanted to, I could not put out of my mind Miriam's demand to him to "charm" me. I tried to act as though I hadn't noticed his outstretched hand and began to walk slowly away from him.

"Where are we going? And what are we to do with the free time I am giving to you?" I said as lightly as possible.

"For a ride," he said without expression. We went to the stables, where Matthew prepared the carriage, chastising us for not having told him so he could have it ready.

As we got into the carriage Michael was very serious and distant. I would have received more attention from a footman. I gave him a hopeful smile, for now that the gaiety had vanished, I regretted my actions. I didn't know what came over me when I was with Michael Barington. No matter how I behaved, I regretted it in the end.

He turned the horses in the direction of Sharpsville, a little town close by. I could not imagine why he chose such a route, for it was not particularly pretty, and often slow-moving wagons blocked the road. He handled the horses very well, and they were going along at a nice trot. So far there had been no wagons, and no sign from Michael that he remembered that I was with him. He could be positively beastly—not that I didn't deserve it, but I did not like it.

I had no idea of what might alter his attitude, so I said the first thing that came to my mind.

"How long have you been at Briarcliff Manor?"

"We arrived about a week before you came home."

He had not bothered to look at me as he spoke. Again I sat not knowing what to say, and feeling horribly uncomfortable. The more he ignored me the more I felt the urge to attract his attention. In desperation, I apologized.

"I'm sorry. I should not have behaved as I did. You had done nothing to warrant my refusal."

I slumped down in a heap when he did not answer. I looked up at him from the corner of my eye, only to see him grinning and his eyes twinkling. Horrible man!

However, my apology did loosen his tongue. We talked of my trip to England, and I found he had also done a lot of traveling before he went to his uncle Charles's farm to help manage it. I thought how similar his position and Darien's were, and yet how different the two men were. Darien was so open and easy to understand, while Michael was nearly impossible to predict. I could not tell from one moment to the next what he was likely to do, or what he thought, or even when he was serious and when he was playing. He seemed to do exactly what he pleased whenever it suited him. I thought it peculiar that he should have come to Briarcliff Manor with Miriam. And I found it even more strange that she was able to tell him what to do.

The wagons had appeared, and we were now jogging and stopping and jogging again in their wake. I expected Michael to wave them aside so that we could go past, but he did no such thing and I was soon gritting my teeth in irritation. I had no idea if he was again teasing me, or if he really didn't care if we remained behind the wagons all the way to town. So I sat in my seat fidgeting in the dust and the quiet that had again overtaken Michael. It would be a hot day in January before I ever got into a carriage with Michael Barington again. He was impossible, and I was once more drawn to thoughts of Darien. If Miriam had wanted someone to charm me away from Briarcliff Manor she would have done better with a more agreeable man than Michael. She was a terrible judge of people.

As though he grew tired of the whole thing, Michael turned the carriage around in the road and went back to the Manor. He let me out in front of the house. He must not have wanted to come in with me, for he refused to let the groom take the horses, saying he would take them to the stables himself. I went immediately to my room to change my clothes. I was thoroughly miffed, and grimy with dust from the wagon that had been in front of us with its hay dragging over the sides and stirring the dry dirt road. I bathed vigorously, thinking I might never come clean, and put on a light-blue muslin dress for lunch. It had grown very warm, and the air felt like midsummer. I checked my appearance in the mirror, suddenly aware that I wanted to look well. Not being certain for whom, I put it down to my wounded pride.

I hurried to the dining room, in danger again of being late. I breezed into the room only to find it unprepared and Jacobs in a flutter setting the table.

"Mercy, Jacobs, whatever is wrong?"

He stood erect, stopping his frantic motions. His face comically rearranged itself into its usual respectful aspect.

"Everything is wrong, miss, positively everything."

"I see, and could you tell me one of the things that has gone wrong—for instance, what has delayed luncheon?"

"It's Aggie, miss. She is leaving, and the whole kitchen staff has gone into an uproar. None of them knows what to do without her."

"*Leaving?* What has caused her to feel that she must leave?"

Jacobs looked helpless, so I walked toward the source of the problem. Before I reached the door to the kitchen, the baleful voice of Aggie came to my ears. She was indeed in a state. Her usually complacent face was twisted into a mass of wrinkled misery.

"Aggie, what has happened? Jacobs said you were leaving."

"Oh, miss, it's true. I must leave. I can't manage another moment here."

"But, Aggie, I was just here this morning and you said the larder was stocked, the wine cellar full, and all was well. What could possibly have occurred in four short hours?"

"How was I to know it weren't true?"

This was getting me nowhere. I took her by the arm and led her to the kitchen table.

"Come here, Aggie, and sit down. Please, Jacobs, bring her a cup of tea . . . and some brandy."

Jacobs stood like a stick, unheeding of me.

"Now, Jacobs, please!" I said more firmly, and he left to do as I bade. "Now, Aggie, start at the beginning. I do not understand any of this."

Jacobs returned promptly with the brandy and the tea, and Aggie reached out gratefully for the snifter. Her eyes began to water dangerously, and I dreaded the prospect of the woman crying. I would never be able to make any sense of this from an hysterical cook.

"Please, Aggie, try to explain it to me."

"It started a while ago, but I wasn't knowing of it. You see, while you was away, I went for a visit to my sister. She has the nicest little farm and I—"

"Aggie, just tell me about the kitchen, for now."

"Yes, miss. Well, when I come back I looked at the kitchen accounts. Everything seemed like it was in order, but I kept missing things. So I asked Bertha—she took over for me while I was gone—and she said it was Mrs. Asherton who moved everything about, and I'd be catching up with things soon enough. I don't like nobody in my kitchen but I knew she didn't know me as yet so I made allowances."

She looked up at me expectantly, so I said, "That was kind of you, Aggie, and very wise."

"Yes." She nodded in complete agreement, and then continued with her tale of woe. "I thought so, too, her being new and all. She come here yesterday, and said she ordered all new supplies, and she give me the lists. She's a great one for lists, all pretty as you please. So when you come in this mornin' I told you all was taken care of. I stretched the truth a bit, but with Mr. Barington here, and so anxious he was to see you and all, I didn't think it would harm. The larder was supposed to be filled in the hour. It weren't a very big stretch . . ."

"It's all right, Aggie, I can understand that, but what is the problem now? What happened?"

"The larder! It's not full. It's just a mite short of empty. She didn't order them things, she just give me the list back. I can't manage a kitchen like this. It ain't like it was with you."

"You mean we have no food or supplies in the larder now?"

"Hardly any."

"Merciful heaven! What could she have been thinking of?"

"She weren't thinking of anything. It were no accident, and I won't stay on in a house that's run like this one is goin' to be. I have my pride, too!"

This last came on a tearful croak. She sat with her arms resting on the table. Her eyes were watering and sad as she sipped her brandy, and ignored the tea.

"Aggie, can you fix any kind of a lunch?"

"I could . . . if I'd a mind to!"

"Well, please do. And I will see to stocking the larder. Send Ernest to me in the morning room. I will give him the list of our needs."

"Yes, Miss Annabel. I'll help you, but I'm leaving the minute she takes over. I'll stay . . . for you, but only till then."

"Thank you, Aggie," I said, patting her plump shoulder. There was no one kinder or bigger-hearted than Aggie, and I knew she meant it when she said she was staying for my sake.

I went into the morning room armed with the lists Aggie had approved for Miriam. I glanced down at them, idly thinking Miriam's handwriting was very untidy. The lists were quite complete, and needed little alteration. I copied them hastily, making a few additions. When Ernest appeared in the doorway some ten minutes later, I was prepared to give him the new list and send him on his way. With relief, I thought Aggie would be well stocked before dinner time.

I sat for a moment collecting my thoughts. I had to decide how to approach my father with this information. For the first time I had something tangible to present to him regarding Miriam. All my previous feelings had been no more than suspicion, but this time I had facts, and the handwritten list as well. I did not know what it all meant, or what Miriam thought she had to gain by such a move, but I agreed with Aggie that it was no accident.

Even so, I would have to be very cautious. My father and I had many long years of experience in disliking each other. He would not take kindly to this information. Perhaps, I thought, I should try a little deceit of my own. I could appear to be innocent, acting as though I didn't know for certain that Miriam was responsible. He would certainly recognize her handwriting. He could reach the obvious conclusion by himself, and I could always come out with the truth if it became necessary.

I walked quickly over to the library. My knock was brisk and firm.

"Come in."

He and Darien were still busy with the farm accounts.

"Father, I would like to speak to you of a matter of some importance."

He seemed to consider for a moment. "Annabel, we are very busy right now. Is it urgent?"

"No, not pressing, but it is something that should be tended to today."

He pulled his watch from its pocket. He made a face, sucking air through his teeth. "We should be finished by two o'clock. I can talk with you then."

He started to turn his attention back to the books, then he looked again at me. "Tell Jacobs to set a luncheon table in here." As an afterthought he looked over at Darien. "You don't mind working as we eat, do you?"

"No, I don't mind," said Darien. "But didn't you plan to go into town?"

"That'll have to keep," Father grumbled. "Tell Jacobs, Annabel."

Darien's eyes had rested on me throughout my conversation with Father, and I found it difficult not to respond to him.

"I'll tell Jacobs, but it may be a while before he serves you. There is quite an upset in the kitchen."

Father looked as though he might ask about it, but thought better and returned to his work.

Somehow Aggie and Jacobs managed to get the kitchen help back in line and produce a delicious luncheon only forty minutes past the normal time. Apparently no one but me, and perhaps Father, had expected lunch at its proper time; I was the only one to appear in the dining room.

I rang a small dinner bell, which we seldom used, and Michael and Clarissa appeared. Miriam did not, and she was not missed. I found myself smiling at the thought of the list I would show to Father, and Clarissa smiled back at me. She was always willing to join in anyone's brighter spirits, whenever they could be found at Briarcliff Manor. I had never seen Clarissa angry or unpleasant. The worst I had ever got from her was a complaint of nothing to do, and I could not fault her for that. The Manor on its best days was oppressive. Father had never been touched by the lighter side of life, and he seldom let it creep into the lives of those around him.

"You and Michael must have had a nice ride," said Clarissa. "You look very happy. I do wish you had asked me to go along. I would love to go out for a while."

"We had a marvelous time," I said looking directly at Michael. "Michael is an accomplished conversationalist."

"Oh, I think so, too. He is so funny."

Very funny, I thought, as Michael turned his attention to Clarissa and asked if she would like to go out in the afternoon. I said cheerily, with my voice too high, "See! You have only to ask and you have gotten your wish."

Clarissa could not have been more pleased, and was not in the least handicapped by any reluctance in showing her pleasure.

I looked away from them, and began to think once more of what I might say to Father.

"What is it you are mulling over, Annabel?"

I looked up at Michael and said it was nothing of importance. He did not appear to believe me, and I wondered if somehow he knew what I was about to do. I did not want Miriam to be forewarned as I spoke to Father, and I could not be certain Michael would not tell her. After we had finished eating and were leaving the dining room, he came over to where I stood.

"I don't know what you are contemplating, but be cautious."

He did not wait for me to reply, and I was not sure of what he meant.

I pushed Michael and his confusing ways from my mind and passed my time by picking some flowers and arranging them in vases for the dining room and the main parlor. The gardens were nearly spent at this time of year, so I had to resort to the greenhouse. I finished my task, stopped long enough to be certain my hair and dress were neat, in order, and then proceeded to the library.

My hand was poised in midair before the door when it opened. Miriam smiled at me as she left the room, sweeping past me with an air of great satisfaction.

"Well, come in, Annabel. Don't stand forever in the doorway. What are you gawking at?"

My father's tone of voice threw me back to the time when he had lived in a constant state of ill humor. I closed the door behind me. I felt the smooth paper of the list I carried in my left hand, feeling the certainty it gave me in proving my accusation. He began to speak immediately as I came in.

"Sit down." He indicated the chair Darien had been sitting in earlier. "What is this nonsense I hear about the error you have made in the kitchen? Miriam tells me the larder is nearly empty, and Aggie and a good portion of the kitchen staff are leaving!"

His breathing was labored, and he paused, but I was so startled at the turn of events that I failed to take advantage of the respite.

"You have not been home for three full days yet, and you have managed to disrupt the entire household. Are you good for absolutely nothing?"

He began to pace the floor.

"Father, I believe if you will look at this list you will see that it was not I who was disruptive in the kitchen, and I might add that had it not been for my intervention Aggie would indeed have left this very noon. As it is, she has promised to stay until after your wedding."

I held out the list to him. His hand shot forward, and he snatched it from my hand. He brought it near to his face and hastily scanned the neat lines of foodstuffs to be ordered. His eyes focused on me again, cold and hard.

"What is this supposed to mean? It is a list of food!"

"But . . . don't you recognize the handwriting?"

"Of course I do. It's Aggie's. Of what significance is that?"

I grabbed the paper back from him. What a fool I was! I remembered thinking the handwriting was of a poor quality for someone such as Miriam, but in my joy of having caught her, I had not thought of Aggie. I had always made the lists out myself and given them to Aggie for a final check, but of course Miriam would not be so foolish as to leave her own handwriting on an unfilled order. I was in the process of realizing how thoroughly Miriam had outfoxed me, when she entered the library without knocking.

She was wearing a look of great sympathy and distress on her face.

"John, dear, I can see you have spoken to Annabel about the problem of the larder. I believe you have been too harsh with her."

"I don't see how it is possible to be too harsh with her. Such a damnably fool stunt like this is inexcusable."

Miriam gave him a look of offended femininity at his choice of words, but continued to speak in her cajoling tones.

"She is young, John, you must try to remember that."

"Young!" he sputtered. "She's a damned old maid, taken to prancing around Europe with men not good enough to marry her, and that is all she will ever amount to. There is nothing you can tell me about my daughter I don't already know. She is just like my wife was." He looked at me, and then back at Miriam.

"Please, John, let's be a happy united family."

I felt she might start drooling pure syrup as she mouthed these words, but my father looked down into her eyes as she stood there patiently, meekly by his side, her hand moving gently back and forth along the sleeve of his coat, waiting for him to bend to her will.

His face softened, and the tone of his voice dropped to one of intimacy.

"But, yes, for you we will let the matter rest."

He put his arm around her waist and drew her into the red leather chair he favored.

"Now let me see . . ." He began to talk to her as though they were alone in the room. For all he thought of me it was true. ". . . How long will it be? Today is Tuesday, and . . ."

I could not stand it any longer. I wanted to scream at him, make him see that it was he who was the fool. At that moment I hated Miriam fervently, and my father as well. I walked from the room still clutching Aggie's list. I don't believe he knew I was gone, but I would have wagered that Miriam not only knew but had watched me leave.

I stumbled out across the hall, hoping I would not meet anyone. I had begun to shake all over, and wasn't certain I could manage the stairs to my room. I stopped for a moment, leaning against the table in the center of the hall.

I met no one, and I don't recall how I got there, but I ended up on the bench in the dogwood garden. Over and over I recalled each detail, each step Miriam must have taken to lead me into my father's library so full of confidence, armed with the list that would vindicate her and make me look like an idiot. I laughed bitterly as I remembered feeling pleased at the thought that she did not know people. She could not have known *me* better.

I have no idea how long I sat there, but I missed tea. Darien had asked for me, and the others had told him they hadn't seen me since lunch. Even before I was told, I suspected this to be the case, for I saw him immediately when he left by the terrace in search of me. I could have remained hidden from anyone else, but Darien already knew my habits too well. After a detour by the stables to see if Bucephalus was still in his stall, he came directly to the dogwoods. I didn't move away.

"So there you are, Annabel!"

I looked up and said lifelessly, "Yes, here I am."

He cocked his head to one side, his forehead crinkled in a mock frown.

"What's wrong? It is too beautiful a day to be unhappy."

I looked about me, and realized it was a beautiful day.

"You are wasting one of the loveliest autumns we have had in years," he continued. "Don't you realize how rare it is to have warmth, greenery, and weather like this so late in the year?"

I agreed with all he said, and asked him to sit down.

Sensing that he had already begun to brighten my mood, he continued talking lightly and inconsequentially until I fell easily in with his banter. It was then he asked me about our ride.

"Have you forgotten our trip around Briarcliff Manor?"

74

"No, of course not, but you have been very busy since I returned."

"Tomorrow I am not busy. Since your father had to put off his trip to the city with Miriam this afternoon, they plan to go early tomorrow morning. That leaves an entirely free day."

"It sounds delightful," I said, meaning it.

"If you have a picnic lunch prepared for us, we can make it a full day."

"That would be no trouble at all, and so much fun."

I felt that he had just thrown me a lifeline, and Darien looked equally pleased.

"Good! It's all settled. Tomorrow we go. We will have to start early or we won't see much of it. As it is, we will have to make at least two or perhaps three outings." His eyes twinkled. "Do you mind?"

I began to reply, reassuring him politely; I had learned so long ago to hide my feelings from men that I found it difficult to break the habit. But today, secure with Darien, I stopped myself mid-sentence.

"You should know that I would stretch it into several outings happily."

I thought the next morning would never come. I changed my mind at least a dozen times as to what I should wear, finally deciding on a soft rose-colored outfit. It was new, and I had bought it while in the clutches of vanity. The rose became me, and the black trim accentuated the curves of my figure. Pleased with my choice, I carefully laid it out for the morning.

I awoke at six o'clock. It was much too early, but I was too excited to get back into bed. I felt like a young girl about to go out with a man for the first time. I heard noises in the hallway, and realized Miriam and Father were leaving for the city. It pleased me to think that for the first time since I had been home, I had completely forgotten about Miriam and Father. It was surely a good beginning for the day.

The minutes dragged themselves across the face of my clock. I was tempted to push the hands up, just to make eight o'clock seem to come faster. I occupied myself by whirling about like a dancer in front of my mirror, admiring the wavering distorted image I saw of a slim young woman in high bloom and looking very smart indeed. Again I admired the rose color of my outfit and made a mental note to use it more often. My boots, polished to a high sheen, matched the subtle sparkle of the jet buttons that adorned the bodice of my dress.

The clock finally cooperated with me and reached the appointed hour. I was ready, and I hurried from my room, dashing down the stairs to breakfast.

Darien was already there. Michael and Clarissa had not yet come down, and I was glad. I took the seat to Darien's right.

"Good morning," he said, and I could see by the look in his eye and the tone of his voice that he liked what he saw. I blushed with pleasure. Darien set before me a dish laden with eggs, fresh warm bread, and ham, but it could tempt only my eyes. I wanted to be on our way, and I ate little. I could not even finish my coffee.

"I hope you have packed a substantial lunch," he said. "That little bit of food you have eaten for breakfast will leave you ravenous by noon."

I laughed and agreed. "I'll undoubtedly gobble up your share of the lunch and leave you ravenous for dinner."

"Try to eat a little now . . . have pity on me."

"I just can't seem to get a bite down. I'm too excited to get started." I dutifully lifted the coffee cup to my lips only to put it down again. "There is so much to see, and you said Briarcliff Manor is so big, and . . ."

He put his hand out to my gesturing one, catching it.

"Whoa . . . We have the whole day. If I had known this trip would have such an effect on you, we would have done it much sooner." His hand pressed more firmly on mine, and I returned the pressure.

"You love Briarcliff Manor, don't you," he said rather than asked.

"I love the place."

He did not catch my reservation, and his hand held mine tightly. His voice was low as he raised me from my seat saying, "Come on, let's go. There is no need to wait any longer."

"What is there no need to wait any longer for?" Michael's bass voice interrupted our mood. Darien dropped my hand and I started.

"We are going for a ride," said Darien. "And there is no need to delay our leaving any longer."

His hand swept the table indicating the empty breakfast plate, and mine that was nearly untouched. Michael gave my plate a cynical look.

"You're rushing her a bit, aren't you?"

"No, Michael, he is not," I answered for myself. "I have eaten quite enough."

The two men were looking at one another. I could not read Darien's expression, but Michael's was for once clear, and it was one of unmistakable dislike.

After an uncomfortable moment he looked over at me.

"When will you be back?"

The question took me by surprise, particularly coming from Michael.

"Why I don't know. We haven't spoken about—"

"It will be late," said Darien positively.

"It will be late," I repeated, wishing only to leave. Darien took me by the arm, keeping me close to him, and led me from the breakfast room.

"I can't imagine what has come over Michael this morning," I said as soon as we were outside.

He took a deep breath, and looked at some distant point before him.

"Well, my dear one, when you get to know Cousin Michael better you will find he can be a most disagreeable chap."

"Really? I found him to be very—"

I hesitated, remembering my encounter with him in the morning room, and his argument with Miriam.

"You found him very what?"

"I was going to say very polite and thoughtful, but I remembered something, and I'm not certain *what* I think of Michael."

The carriage was ready and waiting for us. With his usual efficiency Darien had already seen to it that the picnic lunch was included with a knee blanket and even a shawl for me, in case it turned cooler. And so, on the best of autumn days, we were on our way. The trees were at the height of color in September glory. We had had plenty of rain this year and the lawns as well as the hemlocks were a verdant green, giving the scene of flaming birches and maples a vitality and essence all of their own.

As the carriage moved, Darien and I seemed to become a part of the day. It was as though we had been plucked from out of time and given a day in which we were in complete accord. I could feel it with my whole being. Both of us seemed to have benefited from the absence of Miriam and my father, and the prospect of this special day before us.

For a long while we rode along, the horses going at a leisurely gait. Neither of us felt the need to talk. Darien was sitting relaxed, the reins in one hand and my hand securely in his other. I wondered what he was thinking. He was always so self-contained, and yet a part of whatever he did. I realized that I knew very little of Darien. I rarely could tell what he was thinking, or what he felt. Neither Michael nor Darien made it easy for me to know them, but at least this morning I could see Michael's dislike for Darien. Darien had indicated nothing, then had spoken unkindly of Michael later. It was the same as with Miriam, his words said one thing and his actions another.

I could sense that today we were in close accord with one another, so I decided to ask Darien directly about the things that still bothered me.

"Darien, do you remember the day I first came home?"

He nodded.

"That day I was in my room looking out across the lawn, and Miriam rode to meet someone. Was it you?"

He turned to me, and his eyes were completely frank. "Yes, it was. Why do you ask?"

"Only because it seemed strange—you were mostly hidden by the hemlocks, and Miriam came to you. It was as though you didn't want to be seen."

He laughed. "I was hiding. I didn't do too good a job of it if you saw me, though. Miriam didn't want it known she was preparing to move to the main house before she mentioned it to you and your father. So she had me and her luggage hidden away for the right moment."

"I wondered why Miriam was so certain she could manage that move in so short a time. I was positive she had planned it."

"She had. She usually does."

"Do you know her well, Darien? You seem to." I hoped he would answer negatively.

He rubbed his hand along his jaw as if considering.

"I don't know if you would say I know her well. I met her some time ago, and I know her well enough to know she is a woman who plans, and none of her plans are designed to benefit anyone but herself. She is not a nice woman."

"No," I said. "I don't think she is, and I have felt the results of her planning too often already. But I don't see any point in her schemes. They seem so silly, and I don't see how Father could have chosen her for a wife. I don't remember my mother too well, but I've been told she was a kind and gentle woman."

"She was."

"Did you know her?" I asked him, surprised. "I didn't know you lived at Briarcliff Manor that long ago."

"I've lived on or near Briarcliff Manor all of my life. And yes, I knew your mother. I was quite young, but I remember she was very kind, and a beautiful woman."

"Well, if it is true, don't you think it odd that Father should now choose someone like Miriam?"

His expression changed, and I got the fleeting impression that he did not care for my father. He did not answer me, and I did not press him.

We sat silent again. As we reached the far border of the hemlocks, the land opened again into broad meadows and fields.

"Is this all part of Briarcliff Manor too? It is like another world." I was truly amazed.

"Every bit of it."

He pointed out several fields of grain. Some of them had been harvested, and others were ready for reaping. He chatted on about them, sounding somewhat like a tourist guide. Suddenly he interrupted his monologue.

"Annabel, why do you stay here? It is no place for you to be . . . now."

"Why, whatever can you mean?" I asked, surprised by the abruptness of his statement. "This is my home. I belong here."

My words made no impression on him.

"No, Annabel, you don't belong here. Not any more. Surely you can see Miriam has changed everything. And, Annabel, you have changed, too."

"Oh, Darien, of course you are right. Miriam has changed the Manor, and I know she doesn't want me around, but what can I do? She is going to be my stepmother. And there are other things, too. In spite of my differences with Father, I just can't feel I have the right to run away. I did that before, but I don't feel I can do it this time."

"You don't owe your father anything."

"Perhaps not, but I can't feel that way. I just can't run away again."

"Would you be running away? Or would it be more a matter of leaving an impossible situation?" He seemed to be trying a different approach.

"Is there a difference?"

"Yes, I think there is."

"I don't know. I just don't know what to do. Please let's not talk about it now. Let's be free of Father and Miriam for this one day."

He pulled me closer to him. "You will think about it though, won't you?"

"Yes, I'll think about it. I find it hard to think of anything else."

He turned my face to his. "Try to squeeze in a few thoughts of me."

About an hour later we stopped for our lunch. As slowly as the clock had run this morning, it sped and raced along this afternoon. When we turned back toward the main house it was nearing sunset, and we didn't reach the Manor until it had just turned dark.

As we came toward the house I was surprised to see Michael standing on the terrace quite as if he were waiting for us. As Darien drew the horses to a halt, Michael vaulted down the steps to my side of the carriage. He did not wait for me to rise from my seat, but took me by the waist and lifted me from the carriage.

"Thank you, Michael," said Darien, his voice heavy with sarcasm. "It is kind of you to assist us."

Michael bowed his head in Darien's direction.

"My pleasure," he said, his arm still holding me fast to his side.

Darien said he would see to the horses and left in the direction of the stables.

Michael did not move. He kept me by him. I was feeling awkward, but did not know how to disengage myself without pulling forcibly out of his grasp.

"Did you enjoy yourself?" he asked softly.

"We had a very nice time. I had no idea of the beauty of Briarcliff Manor, or the size of it. The meadows are still green." The mood of the day caught up with me, and my voice lifted with the memory.

"Michael, the colors were magnificent. I don't think there is anything more beautiful than an autumn day such as this one."

As I continued talking, letting the pleasure of the day move in voice, and doubtless in my expression, Michael's hand came up and gently stroked my face.

"There are a few things more beautiful."

He was so gentle I could not bring myself to pull away from him. I just stood there, watching his face as his eyes took me in. I know my cheeks were flushed, but I remained in his grasp, not wanting to behave with him as I had done so often before.

Finally, I could stand his scrutiny no longer. He seemed to notice my discomfort at his actions, for he turned with me toward the house, only to stop once again to point out the moon.

It had just begun its climb and was orange with the warm sunlight color left over from the day. Michael stood behind me, his hands on my shoulders. He leaned forward and kissed the tip of my ear.

Startled, I turned to face him. I felt helpless, but I could not let this continue. I gestured my confusion.

"Michael, please. I don't know what to say . . . but . . ."

"There is nothing to say."

He pulled me against him, held me there close and unmoving. I could feel the rapid beat of his heart. Then his hand came up, tilting my head so that his mouth came down firm and warm on my own. He held me so tightly I couldn't move. I was no longer sure I wanted to, but I prayed that Darien would not return to *this* scene. When Michael finally released me I was gasping for air. I didn't seem able to control my breathing. My chest was heaving, and my head was whirling with unseemly thoughts and desires.

I managed to breathe out the words, "I must go in."

He started toward me again. I was frightened by what I could see in his eyes, and the feelings he aroused in me. I did not know what to do. I had never felt that way before.

"Michael, please. I—"

Clarissa opened the dining room door wide.

"There you are, Michael! I've been looking high and low for you. Oh, hello, Annabel. I didn't know you had come back. Did you—"

I didn't wait for her to finish her question, but ran toward the door she had left open.

"Well, now! What has gotten into her?" I heard her say as I dashed on my way.

I ran for my room. I didn't care how strange I might look to the servants or anyone else who might see me. I shut the door to my room, leaning against it in the dark, trying to catch my breath, which Michael seemed to have stolen permanently from me. For the first time in I don't know how long I flung myself across my bed and cried.

I couldn't say why I cried. There didn't seem to be anything else to do, and somehow I had to let my feelings out. Thinking didn't do me any good. Yesterday I had suspected everyone in the house of being involved in some dishonest plot, and today I could not feel that anyone was suspect of anything. Darien was so honest, how could *he* possibly be involved in anything? He had answered all of my questions without hesitation. Father and Miriam? Both of them were disagreeable people, but they were acting like themselves. Miriam would probably never draw a breath but that it bode evil for someone. What better than that they should be together? They probably understood each other perfectly.

Darien was right. I was the one who was out of place with them. That left Michael and Clarissa as the plotters. No one could suspect Clarissa of anything. She was a flirt, lighthearted and light-minded. Clarissa could not be evil. She was simply herself.

And Michael? What of Michael? Miriam had said he was a

ladies' man, a charmer. But was he really? I didn't know, but I found it hard to believe that his actions on the terrace were part of a calculated campaign to woo me. And why me? No one had ever treated me like this before.

My mind reeled in its confusion. It had been four short days since my return. I had come home a confirmed spinster, wishing only to take advantage of whatever life offered me, and now in one day I had been attracted strongly by two men, each of whom had returned that feeling with an even stronger one of his own.

Thinking was getting me nowhere. Had it been daylight, I would have run to the stables for Bucephalus. I always rode him whenever I had a problem. I loved the feeling of the wind cutting at me, flicking at my hair and rushing through my teeth. But I could not run for Bucephalus now. I promised myself I would ride early in the morning. For now, I cried some more. They were little-girl tears, and I knew well they should have no place in my life.

I looked a sight when I finally stopped sobbing. I couldn't face anyone tonight. Dinner had been planned late, as Father and Miriam were not expected before nine. I had not heard them return, so I knew the others would be waiting for me to come to the library. I rang for Lettie. She came immediately. I did not open the door, but called through it.

"Lettie, please tell Miss Clarissa I will not be down for dinner. Tell her I don't feel well— No! Tell her I have a headache."

"Yes, miss. Do you want a tray brought up here for you?"

"No. I don't think so. Maybe a cup of tea later."

"Yes, miss."

She left and I slumped into a chair, sitting in the dark.

It was probably an hour later when Lettie again knocked at my sitting-room door. This time I opened the door, remembering to light one candle. Lettie came in and set a tray on a small table beside my chair.

"Mercy, Miss Annabel, it's dark and gloomy in here. Let me get you some light."

She busied herself lighting several candles, while I shrank back into the corner, avoiding the revealing light. Finally satisfied, she returned her attention to the tea tray.

"You see, I brought you some cakes . . . just in case you might be feeling a little like eating now."

"Thank you."

"I almost forgot," she said. Her face lit up with a conspiratorial grin. "You have a message, miss. From a gentleman."

My heart skipped its beat, but at that moment I couldn't be sure if it skipped in the hope that the note came from Darien or Michael.

"Thank you, Lettie."

She curtsied. "Are you feelin' better, Miss Annabel? You looked a bit peaked when I first come in, and now you're lookin' flushed. You're not comin' down with a fever now, are you?"

I laughed lightly, then sniffled, and my eyes began to mist again.

"No, Lettie, I'm all right. I am just having an attack of foolishness, and I didn't want to go down to dinner."

She gave me a knowing look. "I understand that, miss. It happens to all us women sometime. And don't forget this." She handed me the note.

"I won't."

She left, to my relief. I did not seem to do anything right. I had just violated the basic rule with servants—not that I had not thrown all my upbringing to the wind at some time today. Lettie would no doubt spread the information that my "gentleman" friend had upset me so I couldn't go to dinner. I could nearly hear the speculation and talk that would enliven the kitchen for the next few days. I brought my fist down on my knee in exasperation. How could I possibly have made such a mess of an orderly, well-disciplined life in four short days!

I looked at the note clutched in my hand. I wanted to read it, but could hardly bring myself to open it. I thought of each of the men who might have sent it. I had just called one of them my gentleman friend; now I wondered which of them I had meant.

I found that I did not know the answer. My head told me I wanted it to be Darien. He had shown me nothing but a steady reliable kindness. There was no rushing at me, or throwing me into wild confusion such as I experienced with Michael, and yet I could be no more certain of Darien than I could of Michael. Miriam had managed to move between each of them and me. I did not trust anyone with whom she seemed close, and both of these men had assisted her in some way. I could not be certain that Michael had not told her of the list, thereby allowing her the opportunity to speak to Father before I was able to. He had had the time, and he had given me that strange warning as he left the dining room yesterday. I turned the note over and over in my hand. Slowly I prodded the envelope open with the tip of my finger. It was very short, and its brevity told me the author before I saw his name.

Dearest Annabel,
I missed you at dinner tonight. Sleep well.

I looked at the words. Lettie would have been sorely disappointed had she known what was in the note. I read them over again, for as few words as there were, they carried much meaning to me of the friend who wrote them.

He had signed his name at the bottom: Darien. As I held the note in my hand, I let his thought for me warm and soothe me. I remembered the whole day just as though it were beginning again, just as he had intended I should.

# 7

WHEN I AWOKE THE NEXT morning, I was feeling much better, and willing for the time being to wait and see what would happen. I had placed entirely too much importance on my exaggerated reactions to what was really a simple kiss from Michael. I was busily telling myself to be mature, and to stop behaving like a dither-headed girl as I walked into the breakfast room. Clarissa looked up at me immediately.

"What are you going to wear tonight, Annabel?"

I looked at her blankly, said good morning to the others around the table, and returned my attention to Clarissa. I felt incredibly stupid and could not for the life of me think why she should be interested in what I might wear.

"I . . . I don't know, Clarissa. I really hadn't thought about it."

"Annabel! How can you be like that? I can hardly wait to go, and here you have not even considered it."

She looked thoroughly astonished and dismayed. I looked helplessly around the table. Michael's face was a concentrated blank, as was Miriam's. Father, surprisingly enough, looked pleasant, and it was he who came to my assistance. Looking at Michael and Miriam, he spoke patiently and with a good deal of tolerance.

"She doesn't remember. It is just like my daughter to completely overlook something that young girls usually look forward to." He then turned his attention to me. "There is a ball at the Hites' tonight. Miriam told you about it the first day you came home."

"She did?"

By now Michael was looking amused, and adding in every way he could to my discomfort. Miriam remained passive.

"Oh, Annabel, you are impossible. How could you have missed hearing Miriam? It's the most exciting thing that has happened around here since I've been here. Probably the only exciting thing around here for ages," Clarissa added with her usual innocent lack of tact.

I began to stammer that I had no idea how I could have missed that part of the conversation, but one more look at Michael's face, and the memories of that first day home, answered me more than adequately. I found myself blushing in remembrance. Michael stood patiently waiting for the color to subside in my face.

"Wouldn't you like to sit down and join us for breakfast?"

It was only then I realized I had remained in the same spot since I first entered the room, and Michael had been standing the whole time.

"Oh, I am sorry, I forgot, I mean I didn't think."

"Sit down, Annabel!" said Father from his seat. He smiled knowingly at the others as if in explanation of his seated position.

"I gave up on her long ago." He shrugged his heavy shoulders and slurped the last drops from his teacup.

After we had finished eating, I sought out Clarissa. Now that I knew we were to go out this evening I wanted nothing more than to look my best, and I wanted someone to share my belated excitement with. There was no one more willing than Clarissa. We went together to my room to rummage through my closet.

"I am certainly glad to see you want to go," she said. "I was beginning to think you didn't care about anything."

"I really didn't hear Miriam say anything about it. I was a bit foggy that day. I wonder what else I missed."

"Michael always has that effect on women," she said matter-of-factly. I began to protest strenuously, but gave up quickly. Clarissa had an intuitive cunning, that would not even consider my protestations, let alone believe them. She was looking at me speculatively.

"You would look best in soft colors, I think. That or something deep and dramatic," she said wisely, and I wondered if I would have been so kind to her.

She rapidly flipped through the gowns I had, and pulled four of them out of the wardrobe. She laid them out on the bed and stepped back, considering each one of them. She eliminated a lavender and a gray one, saying they were too cold and austere. I was fascinated watching her, and said nothing, agreeing with each of her opinions.

For many things Clarissa was worse than having no one, but when it came to being a woman, and knowing how best to display that femininity, I suspected there were few who could outdo her. I thought now nice it must be to be like her, and to have such direct desires, and to be satisfied with them.

"I just don't know . . ." she said. "Either of these would be perfect. Which do you like best?"

She indicated the two gowns remaining. One was pale gold, modestly cut, and sparingly trimmed with a soft draping lace. The other was a deep wine-red velvet. I had never worn it, for the neckline was quite low, and I had never had the courage to appear in it, although I had often worn it in the privacy of my bedroom with my dreams and my mirror as an escort.

"Well, you said I should wear pale colors . . . so perhaps . . ."

She whipped the gold gown from the bed. "I agree!" she said as she replaced it in the closet. "The wine! Definitely the wine. It is by far the prettiest, and it will make your skin glow with color."

She picked it up, smiling broadly. She held it to herself and waltzed about in front of the mirror.

"You will look beautiful, Annabel."

"It isn't too low-cut?"

"Mercy, no! You fret about the silliest things. Now come and see what I am to wear."

We went to her room. There were gowns hanging every-where. The bed was a sea of blues, greens, and pinks. I did not believe I had ever seen so many clothes in one woman's pos-session before. I wondered how she ever traveled. It must have been by caravan.

"I think it will be this one," she said, diving into a pile of silk, and coming up with a delicate embroidered gown the color of a robin's egg. It was dainty, and I could well imagine it on Clarissa, with her gay blue eyes heightened in intensity by the soft colors in the dress. She was delighted by the sound of pleasure that emerged from me.

"Just think of all the men that will be there tonight," she said dreamily.

"I suppose there will be many."

"I just hope some of them will be young. You can never tell with these things that Miriam goes to. She likes older men for some reason." She looked at me, puzzled and concerned. "I don't understand Miriam," she said. "She is attractive enough, and many others whom I would have considered more suitable have tried to court her, but she always goes to the older ones. You know her first husband was nearly seventy-five when she married him. Can you imagine? And she had just turned twenty-two."

"I am surprised he was interested in her."

"What did he care! All he wanted was a good hostess, a wife to put on a good show for him, and make him look like a prosperous man, and a good host."

"I didn't know."

"Oh, my, yes," she said confidentially. "He was in debt up to his ears, but no one knew. He just kept paying off one debt with another. Not even Miriam realized what he was doing, and when he died it was awful. I have never seen her so angry. I thought she would lose her sanity. She was livid, with all those people wanting their money, and her without a penny."

"It must have been very hard for her."

Clarissa made a little noncommittal face as she looked at herself in the mirror. "I don't know. She was married to him for six years, and she lived well. Then she met my uncle, Charles

Asherton, and they were married about a year later. That's not so bad."

"No, I don't suppose so, but I wouldn't like to go through it."

"You would if all you wanted was money. That is why she married him. Uncle Charles, too, I think."

"That couldn't have made it easy for any of you."

"I never liked him. Michael was his favorite."

"Oh," I said blankly. "Was he old, too?"

"Well, not like poor Mr. Beggs, but he was old for Miriam. Uncle Charles must have been about fifty-six or -seven I guess. He was a funny old duck. He either liked you or he didn't, and I came in on the wrong side of him. He never approved of me."

"That's too bad."

"Oh, not really," she answered. "He was nice to me, in his way. I have no complaints. He handled all my parents' money for me as I grew up, and then arranged for me to have a generous living allowance."

She indicated the profusion of gowns. I agreed with her, and she began to put the dresses back into the wardrobe. I helped her to finish, and we parted ways at the doorway.

The remainder of the day passed quickly, and before I knew it, it was time to get dressed. Clarissa's eagerness had rubbed off on me, and I found that I too was looking forward to the evening with enthusiasm. I went into the parlor, where Darien, Father, Miriam, and Michael were waiting for Clarissa and me. I was pleased to note that Clarissa's assessment of my dress had been accurate. I felt beautiful when each of the men, including my father, complimented me. I could not get over my father's good humor today. I could honestly say I had never seen him act so pleasant. It was only five minutes before Clarissa breezed into the room like a breath of spring air. She achieved her effect, and we all prepared to leave.

Mr. Arnold Hite and his wife Nancy lived in a large unstylish square house. The rooms were spacious, but not particularly charming. It seemed the house and all that was in it resembled their owners and maintained an air of stability and squarishness. The only exception was the grounds. All of their creativity had been poured into this endeavor. The road coming up to the house was like a tunnel formed by carefully trimmed bushes, which I could not identify in the darkness. I am certain that some of them were honeysuckle, for I could smell the heavy scent as we passed, but I could not tell what the others were.

When we entered and were announced to the people within, I could not believe my eyes. As we came into the ballroom, Miriam took on a completely different character. Everything about her changed. She moved easily and with grace among the people. She was charming and warm. Had I met her for the first time at this ball, I was certain I would have liked her and been drawn into her influence. If this was what my father knew of Miriam, I could well understand what had attracted him. I puzzled over the difference in her. Was it Briarcliff Manor? Was it I? Was I really as much of a problem as Father had always said? Or was it Miriam herself, that she could call forth the characteristics she desired at will?

I had little more time to observe or consider, for I was whisked off to the dancing area. Clarissa had no need to fret, for there were men by the score of all ages and sizes. I looked about for her, knowing I would see her at her best, but I could not find her. I did not see any of the people from Briarcliff Manor. It seemed that we had parted at the doorway, and had been swallowed up by the various groups of people in the room.

Mrs. Hite was a woman given to incessant activity, and the music was endless. I was getting very tired when Michael appeared from nowhere. Thoughtfully, he took me to get something to drink rather than dancing. Somewhere among the assortment of drinks he found a glass of plain cool water for me, for which I was very grateful. We had just gone in search of a quiet place to sit and talk, when a rather portly gentleman named Brooms took me off again into the music and the dance. Again I lost track of the others from Briarcliff Manor, and Michael disappeared. I refused to dance the next dance and made my excuses, saying I wished to speak to some friends I had noticed.

From across the dance floor I could see Edith Johnson and

Peggy Stewart. I made my way toward them, thankful for the excuse they afforded me. I had been dancing the whole evening, and it was quite warm in the room. Just to sit and listen to others talk would be a pleasure.

Peggy was a friendly woman, and seemed glad to see me whenever she happened to meet me, which was not often. Over the years we had kept in touch sketchily, but I had not seen her since before I had left for my trip to England. Her smile was welcoming and the tone of her voice was warm as she called out to me.

"Annabel! Come sit down, and let me see you."

"Hello, Peggy," I said, as always taken aback by her effervescence.

"You have become a stranger to us," she continued, with her face lighting with the subject she was about to pursue. "Whatever do you mean chasing off to England without so much as a word to your friends?"

"Hello, Annabel," interjected Edith in the midst of Peggy's words. "I only found out tonight that you had gone to England, and now here you are back again already."

"I'm sorry, Edith, I suppose I should have told everyone, but it came about suddenly. A friend of mine suffered a tragedy, and needed someone to accompany her. I just made up my mind to go, and did not think of mentioning it. It was selfish of me. The next time I go anywhere I'll be sure to mention it to you."

"But you are going back, aren't you?" asked Peggy looking slightly bewildered.

"Well, I suppose I shall someday, but I have no idea when it might be."

Peggy and Edith looked at each other.

"What is wrong?" I asked.

"Nothing probably," said Edith. "It is just that we were told you were planning to take a trip in the very near future." Edith paused and looked over at Peggy once more, then she continued. "Miriam seemed very definite about your plans, and we thought she would surely know . . . if anyone would."

"Miriam told you I was leaving for Europe again? In the near future?"

"Yes. I'm certain we understood her correctly. After all, both of us would not have been mistaken, would we, Peggy?" Edith looked at Peggy for verification.

I had no idea what to make of this, nor could I think of anything to say. Seeing my predicament, Peggy came to my aid gallantly, but her expression was not one that I enjoyed seeing. She was troubled and could not hide it.

"Annabel, I don't think it was anything to worry about. You probably mentioned returning one day, and Miriam misinterpreted. That does happen sometimes."

Edith jumped in to add her own bit of consolation. "Oh, my, yes! Things like that happen all the time. Why, when you were gone the last time we thought you were dead and gone. That Briarcliff Manor is so isolated out there a body never knows what is going on."

"Edith!" cried Peggy. "Hold your tongue. I've never known a woman who could run on like you can."

"It's all right, Peggy," I said. "Briarcliff Manor is isolated, and I'm afraid we have always been negligent about telling people what is happening in our lives. But when was it that Miriam told you about my upcoming trip?"

"Oh, that was some time ago. Nearly a month, I'd say."

"I didn't know Miriam then . . . I had never even spoken to her then." I said in a near-whisper, more to myself than in answer to Peggy.

"What did you say? I didn't hear," Peggy said leaning toward me in an effort to hear me. I did not repeat myself.

Edith had been sitting quietly and thinking to herself. She was no longer to be kept from voicing her thoughts by any effort of Peggy's or mine. I had often avoided Edith for this very reason. She always had had an inordinate curiosity about Briarcliff Manor, and the people who lived and worked there. She would ask me anything that came to her mind as though I were not one of those living there, but just another woman, who would naturally be as curious as she.

"You certainly are tight-lipped about that place. Everyone is. It has always made me wonder . . . it is positively spooky, and the people you have out there! It's enough to send chills up your spine."

I mentally shook myself free of my own spooky thoughts about Miriam. "Edith, really. I think you exaggerate. Briarcliff Manor may be far from the other houses, and in the country, but it is hardly spooky, and as far as people go, I am one of them, and no one has ever thought me spooky before tonight. Unless you mean the servants, the only other people who live at the Manor are Miriam, my father, and Darien Varka."

"Edith you are being ridiculous, not to mention rude," added Peggy.

"Well," sniffed Edith, "Mr. Varka is enough by himself to frighten me to my grave.

"Darien?" I asked in great surprise. "He is one of the nicest men I have ever known," I said. "Whatever could be frightening about him?"

"I'd like to know what could frighten you about him, too. I think he is charming, and very handsome," said Peggy, delighted with the thoughts Darien stirred in her mind.

"Nice! Charming! I can see neither of you knows him well, and neither of you has seen him when he is angry, have you?" stormed Edith, piqued by our reactions.

"No," I replied. "I have never seen him angry, and I don't think it is in his makeup. He is a very level-headed man."

"There isn't a man alive incapable of anger," said Edith smugly.

"I didn't mean *ever* angry. You implied a severe anger, and I don't believe he would be that way."

"Well, I most certainly do. He is a positive madman!"

"Honestly, Edith," said Peggy, out of patience. "I think you have confused him with someone else."

"I have not! There he is, standing right over there with Miriam and Elmer Berger."

We all turned in the direction she indicated. Darien was indeed standing with Miriam, and the man Edith had named as Elmer Berger. His head was thrown back in laughter, and his lean figure showed to perfection in the neatly tailored suit that he wore. Peggy with her usual enthusiasm spoke to Edith without taking her eyes from Darien.

"The only thing frightening about that man is his appallingly good looks. I think you are the one who is mad. He probably has simply ignored you all night, and you have not yet recovered."

"Don't be ridiculous. I would rather sit on this chair all evening than dance one dance with him."

"I'm sure," Peggy replied.

Edith looked at both of us as though we were dense and stupid. "You don't understand," she said more softly. "I know what I'm saying. I—"

"Oh, let's not talk of unpleasantries tonight. I'm sure you have cause to think him bad tempered," Peggy said with finality as she looked directly at Edith. Unsatisfied, Edith closed her mouth into a small rigid line, and said no more except by the expression in her eyes.

At that moment, a gentleman I did not know stepped up to Peggy, asking her if she would like some refreshment. She was grateful for his interference and went off with him, leaving Edith and me sitting in silent disagreement over a subject neither of us wished to pursue.

I caught Darien's eye, and he came to my rescue. He cordially bowed to Edith, and asked if she would care to accompany us. Casting a meaningful glance at me, she refused.

"I have hardly seen you all evening," he said, smiling down at me.

"I know, I was thinking the same thing. There are so many people here, I am afraid I have already forgotten many of the names of the people I have been introduced to."

"I doubt that any of them have forgotten yours."

I blushed slightly and was pleased.

We went toward the garden door, thankful for a breath of cool air. Mr. Hite's gardens were quite renowned, and I peeked out of the door to see if I could get a glimpse of them from where I stood.

"Would you like to go into the rose garden?" Darien asked. "It is just outside this door."

"They are not still in bloom, are they?"

"A very few of them, but it is still very pretty. Come along, I will show you."

We placed our glasses on a small table near to the door and

went into the garden. It was just as Darien had said, still very beautiful. I could well imagine what it had been earlier in the summer. The roses were in neat rows that formed paths. In the middle of the garden was a large trellis, more of an arbor, over which the roses climbed. It led to a small circular summerhouse buried beneath cascading roses. The flowers were nearly spent and we walked along paths laden with the petals that had fallen. It was like walking on a pink fragrant cloud.

We went into the summerhouse, and sat on a small bench that had been placed there. There was the slightest of breezes, and it rustled softly through the leaves, every now and then carrying a leaf or a petal with it. It became a kind of a game watching the petals being caught by the wind, and wondering which would survive the gust, and which would silently fall at its gentle force. I have no idea how long we sat there entranced by the quiet, the odor, and the wind, but I had no desire to leave the spell this place cast on me.

I thought to myself that I should impress in my mind every detail of the garden, for I would like to have one like it at Briarcliff Manor.

"It is peaceful here," Darien said softly. "It takes you away from all the things outside."

The moonlight filtered through the open lattices. I could hardly make myself reply to Darien. I was content to sit and let the soft diffused light and the fading scent of the roses work their magic on me. But I looked over at him and replied with my voice barely above a whisper.

"It is like that. But I wouldn't have thought you were one to want to be away from the outside.

"I think everyone wants to get away sometimes. There are always things that press in on one. Things that just won't leave us alone, but we would like to leave them."

He looked at me to see if I had understood his meaning. I tried to reassure him, for his thoughts had disturbed the calm restful mood we had entered. In truth, it was only his words I understood, but I was certain he was thinking of a specific problem that bothered him, and I did not understand. I understood only that the lives of the people with whom I shared my home were troubled and complicated, and each step I took in getting to know them better drew me closer to hostilities which I could neither identify nor understand.

I was quickly becoming disturbed by my turn of thought when Darien turned to me, apparently having dismissed whatever problem had momentarily disturbed him. He turned in his seat to look fully at me.

"This place suits you well. You are like it is, at peace and away from other things."

I was most perplexed by his statement and the intensity of it. I had seen Darien act this way before, the other day on our trip, but now I did not feel comfortable. I had expected him to kiss me that day, or in some way make known the feelings which seemed to ring so clearly in his voice, but he had not. Tonight he was again showing that peculiar, deeply personal intensity, and I wondered what would happen. I could feel the rate of my heart speed up, and I allowed my thoughts to show in my face when I replied to him.

"I like the garden very much. I am glad it was you who has shown it to me. Wouldn't it be nice if we could have one like it at Briarcliff Manor?"

"I think we could do that easily enough. Your garden. I'll speak to the gardener tomorrow morning, and he can make arrangements to have it taken care of."

"As simply as that?"

"Not so simple for Carson, but as simply as that for you and me."

He smiled as he said this last, and then his face grew serious. "For some the path is laid long before they are born, and for them it is always simple."

He stood up and took my hands, raising me from my seat. Before I knew it I was in his arms, and he kissed me gently on the lips. For something I had anticipated for so long, I was ashamed at my reaction to it. My mind immediately went to thoughts of Michael. There was such a difference in the two men.

Darien's arms were about me, and only a moment ago he had kissed me, and all I could feel was that he was very self-contained. Whatever I meant to him, it was locked deep

100

within him, where I could not reach it. I could not tell if it was a kind of shyness that exhibited itself only at moments such as these, or if it were a kind of arrogant certainty that his own feeling was all that mattered, and in some way related to what he had said earlier about things being simple and predetermined for some. I did not know, but I was disappointed and painfully aware that I could not break through whatever it was that seemed so clear to him.

He stood completely at peace, with his arms about me. He was looking at the summerhouse, and his mind was completely occupied with the measurements which he went over one by one, estimating and committing to memory all the pertinent information he would give to Mr. Carson, our gardener, in the morning.

"It will not be difficult to make a garden similar to this one at Briarcliff Manor."

"I'm glad," I said flatly.

He did not seem to notice my tone, for all his enthusiasm was contained in his thoughts. He looked down at me again, and again that peculiar look came over his face. In any other man I would have known it to be a look of desire or passion.

"I'll remember this night and this garden always." His voice was soft and intimate. "Yours will be built by the spring. I'll always know where to find you then."

He tightened his grip on me, and brought me close against him. Then he released me, saying we had best return to the house. "People will begin to wonder where we are."

"Yes," I replied, trying not to show my confused feelings. "I am ready to go back. It is getting chilly now." A shiver ran through me.

His look was one of concern, and he put his arm protectively around my shoulders. We walked back along the path that I had thought a fragrant pink cloud when we had first come out, but now I saw it only as the moribund remnants of a spent summer.

As we reentered the ballroom, Father, Michael, and several other men were coming out of a room off to the left. Judging from the laughter that spilled out after them, it was a room specifically for men. As they saw Darien and me, they came up to us. Father asked if we were ready to leave. We both agreed that it was time. Michael and Darien went off in search of Miriam and Clarissa.

"Have you enjoyed yourself, Father? You look as though you have spent a pleasant evening."

"Indeed I have," he said as he adjusted some cigars Mr. Hite had given to him.

When he had finished his task he walked with me toward the entry hall, and Michael and Clarissa were already there waiting for us. We had just finished thanking our hosts and making our goodbyes when Miriam and Darien joined us. It seemed they had given their thanks before joining us, so we were ready as a group to leave.

The ride back to Briarcliff Manor was quiet. We had left the laughter and gaiety with the Hites and their guests in the ballroom, and it did not take long before the more unpleasant aspects of our lives overtook me. Both Miriam and Darien had disturbed me this evening, and I had not considered them for long during the ball, but now they came back to me. I wished Edith had told me what had happened to make her afraid of Darien. Peggy and I had prevented her from speaking. Now I regretted our haste. I was sure I could have ascertained whether Edith's story was one of imagination mixed with truth, or if it were indeed an accurate appraisal.

Miriam had also disturbed me, for she was not the same person tonight that she normally was at Briarcliff Manor. I could not comprehend how one person could be so completely different, and the announcement of my "planned" journey was inexcusable. A small frightened part of me hoped that her announcement was nothing more than a tasteless way of expressing her desire that I should not live at Briarcliff Manor after her wedding.

I was too tired to sort out my thoughts, but I could sense that I was becoming more and more involved in some scheme of Miriam's that I knew nothing about, except that she wanted me out of the way. The only thing I was sure of as I climbed the stairs to my bedroom was that I was not leaving Briarcliff Manor.

I SLEPT SOUNDLY THAT NIGHT and woke early the next morning feeling much refreshed, but no clearer in mind or heart. The sun was coming up over the East Lawn. I would have time for a nice long ride before anyone else awakened. I hurried through my toilette and dressed in my riding habit. It was only a matter of minutes until I was in the stables. There had not been a sound in the house as I left.

Matthew was moving about in the stable. He did not look so sleepy this morning as he had the last time I came to get Bucephalus.

"Good morning, Matthew. Would you please get Bucephalus ready for me?"

"Are you goin' out ridin' alone again, Miss Annabel?"

"Yes, Matthew. There's no need to worry. As long as I'm riding Bucephalus, there is little chance of anything happening."

"Now that's just not so, miss. I mean no disrespect, but sometimes I think if God blinked his eyes while you was on a horse it'd be the end of you."

"Matthew! What an unkind thing to say. I've been riding for years."

"Maybe so . . . but it hasn't improved you much. It's only God and that horse's love for you that saves you."

"Fiddlesticks, Matthew! You go get my horse for me."

He went off toward Bucephalus' stall, returning soon with the horse in hand.

"Now listen, miss! You be careful. I don't like you ridin' alone. And you take it easy with this horse. You haven't been home for a long time, and there is something wrong about him."

"Oh, no, Matthew! Why didn't you tell me? Is he sick? He doesn't look sick, or—"

"No, it isn't that, he isn't sick. I'm not sure but something is wrong about this horse. He doesn't act right. You just be mighty careful."

"I'm relieved," I said, stroking Bucephalus' neck. "I thought something was really wrong."

"Now you heed me, miss! I'm tellin' you something *is* wrong. Now you listen to me."

I waved my hand at him.

"You're an old hen, Matthew. He was just fine the other day."

He did not reply, but his face remained a mask of disapproval as I rode off.

Perhaps it was Matthew who had upset me, but I felt wary as I rode across the lawn. Bucephalus was edgy this morning and, to be truthful, he had been jittery on our first ride. I thought it simply a result of my extended absence. Matthew had assured me that he had been ridden regularly and given plenty of exercise. Darien had ridden him as often as possible, and had taken complete charge of him for the two weeks prior to my return. It might be that the horse simply did not like the difference in our hands and weight, though I had never known Bucephalus to be so touchy.

I pushed these thoughts to the back of my mind as we picked up momentum. I could never dwell on problems for long once I felt the motion of the horse, and the wind clipping by us. The earth and all my worries were swallowed up in great gulps with Bucephalus' long stride. Little by little, the power of the horse took possession of me, and I felt I was one with him, controlling and masterful.

We reached the end of the open lawn in what seemed but seconds. Bucephalus' stride was even and smooth, beating a wonderful rhythm over the firm ground.

As we entered the trees, I leaned closer to his body for fear of low-hanging boughs. Bucephalus knew me well, and I barely touched the rein to head him in the direction of my favorite path. It was wide and clear, allowing us to race freely toward a gentle curve in the lane. It would be moments before we rounded that curve and came upon an old stone wall that bordered a tiny brook. It was a relatively easy jump, but it was the one I liked best. My knees tightened against Bucephalus' sides in anticipation of the rise of the big horse's weight as he flew across the wall and the water.

I always took that wall in my mind a dozen times before Bucephalus actually cleared it. For me the jump never diminished in excitement. It was an assault on my emotions, fear and power mixing with elation as we lifted from the ground, horse and rider one.

The wall was in sight now. I braced myself, waiting for that moment. Bucephalus' hooves were beating the ground like thunder pelting a dark night.

Without warning he shied, skittering sideways in sharp uneven motions. I fought to keep my seat, but Bucephalus came to a dead halt, and I somersaulted over his head. The world spun as I was flung through the air. I hit the ground with a thud and lay there, unable to move. The sharp tight agony of windless lungs stabbed through me as I struggled to regain my breath. I lay there trying to calm myself, but the panic rose within me as I struggled to breathe.

When at last I could gasp a little air, I tried to move. I moved my limbs as cautiously as possible. My head hurt where it had hit the earth, but I seemed to be all right. I got to my feet, carefully testing each wobbly motion, and walked slowly back and forth until I was satisfied no real damage had been done.

I looked around to see Bucephalus standing on the other side of the brook, waiting for me. Here was the first tangible sign that Matthew's appraisal of Bucephalus had been accurate. I couldn't let him balk at a jump, particularly this one, *our* jump since the first year I had owned him. He was a fine jumper, and this change could not be explained away as a little case of horse nerves.

I started toward him, stiffly, sloshing through the brook and paying no heed to my boots. He was still very jittery; I stroked his golden nose and talked to him as soothingly as I could. We walked back and forth, coming up to the wall several times. I then remounted him and followed the whole procedure again. He seemed to be calming, and I was certain we were ready for another, this time successful, run at the wall. I turned him back down the pathway.

We moved away from the wall until we came to the curve in the lane. Here I turned him around to begin again. Heading toward the wall, he reached a full canter. I was as prepared as I could be for him to shy again, but he showed no sign of doing so—he was heading straight for the wall, picking up momentum as he went. I tried to hold him in check, but he seemed to be going by his own design. Never before had I felt the bold rankling fear that mingled with the anticipation of this jump. I drew in my breath, trying to fasten my imagination on the thought of the mythical Pegasus, as though Bucephalus would become winged also, soaring upward.

He stopped dead. I flew through the air wildly and landed in a crumpled heap. I remember flashes of green and blue whirling by me, then blackness and quiet.

I do not know how long I lay there, but when I opened my eyes Michael was there. His face was worried, and he had me cradled in his arms. I tried to speak his name, but nothing came out. For the moment I could not get my bearings, couldn't think why Michael was there. Then I remembered Bucephalus, and jerked up from Michael's arms.

"Bucephalus . . . where is he?"

"He's all right, Annabel. He's right over there."

I twisted around to look where he had pointed. Bucephalus

stood just where he had stood after our first attempt at the jump. I started to get up.

"Lie still, Annabel. You don't know what you are doing. You've taken quite a fall. Just lie quiet for a while."

"I can't! I can't let him balk. He has to jump that wall. Let me go, Michael!"

He tightened his grip on me, and his voice was crisp, brooking no argument.

"Stay still! You're not getting up on that horse again. I don't know why you weren't killed. Can't you see he is not going to take that jump?"

I tried to sound as matter-of-fact as I could.

"He has never done that before. We always take this path, and he's jumped this wall hundreds of times."

"Perhaps, but he won't jump it today, and you are not going to mount him again."

I was struggling with him when we both heard the approach of another rider. It was Darien. He leaped from his horse and ran to our side.

"Annabel, are you all right?"

"I'm fine," I said with more assurance than I felt. After my first attempt to rise, I was beginning to feel the effects of my fall.

"What happened?"

"Her horse balked at the jump and threw her," said Michael.

"Darien," I said. "You know Bucephalus. He has never done this before. Help me to explain to Michael how important it is that I make him take this jump now."

Darien seemed to consider. We glanced over at Bucephalus and then at me. He started to speak, only to be interrupted by Michael.

"She's not getting on that horse again!"

I wondered how Darien would respond to the finality in Michael's voice. I wasn't certain what I wanted him to do. The longer I lay in Michael's arms, feeling cared for and protected, the weaker was my desire to get back on Bucephalus.

Michael's and Darien's eyes were locked in a battle of wills. It seemed to me that Michael must feel himself to be at a disadvantage, for he was on his knees beside me. It was not a position from which I would have expected a man to challenge another.

"Lead her horse back to the Manor," said Michael. "I'll take Annabel back on mine." Darien was standing with his feet spread wide and seemed talller than he actually was as I looked up at him from the ground. His eyes were hard, and the line of his mouth straight and firm. I wished I had been able to know what he was thinking, for he stood for some time without saying a word. Whatever was going on inside of him, he had not surrendered that to Michael.

I knew Darien would do as Michael asked, but at the same time I could feel the intensity of the current between the two men and I wondered what caused them to be constantly at odds with one another. I never had actually seen them argue or show anger any stronger than they were showing right now. It was more a case of each carefully and warily watching the actions of the other.

As soon as Darien turned and went to get Bucephalus, I forgot my curiosity at their behavior. I sank back into Michael's arms, all of the fight and the desire to ride the horse gone out of me. I felt the muscles in his arm tense to receive my weight, and was happily aware of his strength. He held me there a minute, my face buried in his jacket. I relaxed, secure in being held by him, listening to him. Feeling myself swung upward as he lifted me from the ground, I slipped my arms around his neck and rested my head on his shoulder. Both of us started when we heard the wild screams of a horse.

Michael whirled in the direction of the sound. Bucephalus' head was working up and down as he pawed viciously at the ground. As Darien moved in toward him, he reared. His great body heaved into the air, thrashing wildly about, his hooves ripping at the space above Darien's head. Darien reached for the reins, frantically trying to gain control of the horse. I heard him curse as Bucephalus came down, crowding in against him. Again Darien lunged forward, grabbing for the reins as Bucephalus began to prance, edging sideways.

Whenever Darien moved so did the horse, crowding him

into the wall. The reins dropped from Darien's hand as he quickly moved away. The horse was now a lethal adversary, and it was all he could do to get out of his way. Bucephalus' head was bobbing up and down, and his eyes were crazed with fear. Again Darien made a quick move away from him, and Bucephalus' forelegs rose up into the air, thrashing dangerously close to Darien's head as he leaped the wall into the brook. Bucephalus reared yet again, snorting and pawing, then turned and galloped off.

When Darien climbed the wall to come toward us, he was limping.

"Are you all right? What about your leg? Did he hurt you?"

My questions all ran together.

His attempt at a smile was shaky.

"I'm all right," he said, and wiggled his foot. "But Bucephalus is no gentleman today . . . and he is heavy."

"You're sure that foot is all right?" Michael asked.

Darien nodded, then stood for a moment regaining his breath and his composure. He looked at Michael and me.

"Has that horse ever behaved like that before?"

I reassured him immediately.

"Good heavens, no, Darien. You know him as well as I do. He has always been a gentle horse, and very easy to handle."

He scratched his chin. "I don't understand what got into him. Well, we might as well get back. He's probably halfway home by now. You know how Matthew is—when he sees that horse come in riderless he'll have the whole county out looking for you."

I laughed and agreed.

Darien turned and limped over to his waiting horse. Still holding me in his arms, Michael took me to his. Darien rode off in a rush of thundering hooves to allay Matthew's fears, while Michael kept his horse moving at a slow, even walk. I knew it would take us a long time to return at this pace, but I can't say I minded. I didn't try to analyze my feelings; I just settled against Michael's chest and rode home with him completely in command.

He didn't speak until we reached the edge of the East Lawn.

"Annabel, are you certain Bucephalus has never behaved like this before? You're not just trying to protect the horse, are you? I know you are very attached to him."

"Michael, I am certain he has *never* behaved like that before, and if he were that kind of a horse, I would not be so attached to him—nor would Jules ever have picked him for me."

"He isn't even mildly skittish?"

"No. I've told you; why do you keep asking? You think something is wrong, don't you?"

He laughed at me. "Yes, I'd say something was wrong today."

"That isn't what I meant, and you know it. I mean *really* wrong."

"No. I had no reason for asking. It just seems odd to me that a horse you know so well would act as Bucephalus did. Who handles him?"

"I don't really know. Matthew, I suppose, but it might be any one of the grooms, and Darien exercised him while I was away."

"Do you mean that horse is used to Darien, and still behaved as he just did?"

I didn't answer for I had no suitable reply. I pushed the question from my mind and snuggled closer to Michael. I could not see his face, but I could feel him smile.

"Michael, why were you out riding so early this morning?"

He took my hand and kissed it.

"I might ask you the same question. You are not an easy little lady to catch up with." He looked down at me and smiled. "You and all your headaches and enamored men . . . and horses too. I am forced either to stand in line or to rescue you."

"Oh, Michael, will you be serious for one moment. Why were you out this morning?"

"Because Matthew burst into my bedroom and dragged me out in search of you. He had some unkind things to say about Bucephalus and your ability to handle him, and told me where I'd most likely find you."

"Matthew went right into your room and woke you up? Oh, I am sorry. He should never have done that. I don't know what could have possessed him."

"He did it because he was worried about you. And I'm not sorry. You'd still be out there trying to jump that wall. You know you have no sense, don't you?"

I gave him a reproving look out of the corner of my eye.

He smiled as he brushed his cheek against my own, and I became aware of the faint masculine odor of bay rum.

"You need someone to look after you."

"It seems," I said tartly, "I have several self-appointed protectors. I'm surprised Matthew didn't wake the entire household."

The horse wandered aimlessly and finally stopped as Michael kissed me, a long, tender kiss. I felt no inclination to move away from him as his lips touched my eyes, my cheek, and moved again to my mouth. I wasn't certain what I felt for Michael, but I wanted to let things take their natural course. And Michael was a "natural" man. I did not feel with him that reserve and coolness I sensed in Darien. I needed someone I could share my feelings with, and not merely my words, and Michael did indeed feel—he called from me every ounce of emotion I had to give. I wanted the support and the security of Michael; whatever was afoot at Briarcliff Manor was too strong for me alone.

Perhaps Darien, too, was unable to understand what was happening, or perhaps, if I was wrong in my suspicions, he was too sensible to indulge my runaway imagination. But I leaned close to Michael, feeling happy and peaceful. He was not too sensible to indulge me, and, I thought, probably not too good. Somehow even that thought comforted me, for if I ever came to the point of confiding in someone, Michael would not think me overimaginative or overwrought.

When we came up to the house, Matthew ran toward us. His face was white and covered with perspiration.

"Are you hurt, miss?"

I smiled, eager to reassure him.

"I'm fine, Matthew."

The muscles in his face relaxed, and he crossed himself hastily.

"Thanks be, I'd never forgiven myself. I told you, miss, something isn't right with that horse."

Michael dismounted and helped me down.

Matthew took Bucephalus, mopping at his brow as he led the horse away.

Michael walked me into the house and up to my room. Mercifully we met no one on the way. I could well imagine the scenes that might have followed if we had. Matthew had called a full alarm. But we came uneventfully to my room, and he stood in the doorway.

"Now, my love, you go in and lie down. I'll send Lettie with plenty of hot water, and some very smelly liniment. You are going to be a mighty sore young lady."

I smiled and nodded in agreement. I could already feel the truth of that statement.

"Thank you, Michael," I said softly. "Thank you for being there."

He kissed my cheek lightly. I backed away.

"Not here! Someone will see."

"Let them." His dark eyes were bright with mischief as he moved toward me.

"Michael!"

He grinned at me. "I just thought I'd prefer to kiss you before Lettie puts that liniment on you. You won't smell half as nice afterward."

"Is it that bad?"

He held his nose, then kissed me quickly and said he was going to the stables to talk to Matthew and look at Bucephalus. I felt cheered by his antics, but as I watched him go I wondered what theory about Bucephalus' behavior he might have.

I needed no urging to lie down. Lettie came quickly with steaming hot water and the evil-smelling liniment. She helped me prepare for my bath and get into bed, wondering if I'd ever move freely again. There didn't seem to be an inch of my body that lacked its own individual ache.

Soon I was sound asleep.

# 9

THE NEXT MORNING THE house was buzzing with activity. I walked gingerly down the stairs and made my way to the breakfast room. Everyone was there, which was unusual as it was quite early.

"Well, Annabel, it has been a long time since we've seen you," Miriam said as I entered the room. "I hear you had quite an accident yesterday. You really should be more careful."

I didn't have the energy to spar with her this morning, so I ignored her comments and turned to the pliable Clarissa.

"Good morning, Clarissa. You look bright and fresh today."

Having lost my jealousy of her, I could now enjoy her.

Clarissa smiled sweetly and thanked me. She then looked at each of the men in turn to see if she had the same effect on them. I smiled to myself. Clarissa would be an inveterate flirt at ninety.

Ignoring Clarissa, Miriam gave me a penetrating look.

"Annabel," she said, "I think—that is, your father and I feel—that you should leave the horses to better riders."

"It wasn't her fault," said Michael. "The horse hasn't been tended to properly. She had no way of foreseeing his behavior."

His glance took in both Darien and my father as he spoke.

113

"What do you mean?" I asked. "In what way was he ill attended, Michael?"

His look indicated that he did not want me to pursue the subject.

"It's nothing to worry about. I'll tell you later."

Miriam had risen from her chair.

"Oh, John, my poor dear, I have forgotten your tea."

"Just ring for Jacobs and let him take care of it," said my father. "I can't tell one kind of tea from another anyway."

"But, John, I want you to have my special tea, the herb tea."

"May I have some, too?" asked Clarissa. "If you're going to fix some for John?"

"Of course," Miriam said as she went toward the kitchen. She turned at the doorway and looked back at Clarissa.

"You don't care for the herb tea, do you, Clarissa?"

Clarissa's reply was obvious in her expression.

Miriam let out a long sigh.

"Never mind, I'll fix some other for you."

When Miriam returned with the two cups of tea, she continued speaking to me as though she had not been gone for nearly ten minutes.

"In spite of Michael's opinion, Annabel, I think you should be most cautious. Horsemanship does not seem to rank among your accomplishments."

"I am not a child, Miriam, and I have been riding for years. As you can see, I was not really hurt. You have no need to concern yourself with my welfare."

She shrugged her shoulders. "As you like," she said. "But today we have other concerns."

And so we did. There were four days remaining in which to prepare for the great event. The entire household staff was in full swing, cleaning already clean rooms and furniture. Every downstairs room was turned topsy-turvy, and each of us was asked to assist in some way. Due to my condition I was given the task of helping with the silver. Michael did duty as a furniture mover, along with Jacobs and Ernest. Clarissa was to be in the kitchen with Aggie, and I could not imagine that Aggie would thank Miriam for *that* arrangement.

114

Miriam, I gathered, was to be everywhere. Only Darien and my father were to be left with their normal duties.

Father made a hasty exit, muttering something about having to go into town. Michael jumped to his feet and reached Father at the doorway. He spoke in a very low tone, and I could distinguish none of the words. Whatever it was, he had my father's full attention and displeasure. Apparently there was yet another conflict among the people at Briarcliff Manor that I had not known of. I felt as though I had been away from home for a dozen years.

The expression on Michael's face was intense, and I leaned forward in my seat as far as I dared. I caught a phrase and realized the conversation had something to do with the lawyer Father had gone to see with Miriam yesterday. Just as I began to think I would find out what it was all about, Father shrugged his shoulders and said, "There is not a thing you can do about it."

He left, his expression triumphant.

Michael stood in the doorway for a moment, obviously very angry. Then, as always, he seemed to shake the anger off and go on about his business.

Darien was lingering over his food, and I realized that he wished to speak to me. So I, too, stayed where I was, drinking my coffee very slowly. When the others had left, Darien bent over my chair. He put his hands on my shoulders; his eyes swept over me, and his face showed concern.

"Are you certain you are all right? With Barington there yesterday, I couldn't get near you. I was worried."

"I'm fine, Darien. Truly, there is nothing wrong with me except my sore muscles."

"You'll be aching for several days, I'm afraid. I have some good liniment if you'd like it. But it doesn't have a pleasant odor."

I laughed. "No, thank you, to the liniment. I've had a treatment with that, and one is enough. I shall just have to hobble about like an old woman for a few days."

"I should never have let this happen, Annabel!"

"You? What could you have done? It was my own fault.

Matthew warned me about Bucephalus, and I paid him no mind."

"Mathew warned you? What did he say?"

"Well it was nothing much . . . just that Bucephalus was not himself, jittery or different in some way. He didn't seem to know exactly."

He seemed to relax. "Yes, that's what I thought, too. But I should have been the one to warn you—or to go with you."

Somehow I didn't think he had said what he meant at all.

"I would have liked that. Perhaps next time we can ride together."

He took my hand. "After what happened, you would mount that horse and ride again, wouldn't you? You have a lot of courage, Annabel."

"It isn't courage, Darien. I just couldn't turn my back on Bucephalus."

"Then the next time you ride, I'd like to be with you." Again he looked worried. "Annabel, don't let anything happen to you. Don't stay here."

I released my hand from his grasp.

"Darien, nothing is going to happen to me. I've lived an uneventful life for twenty-four years, and I will continue to do so. There is no need for your worry. You are beginning to be as bad as Matthew."

He started to speak, but I cut him off.

"And, Darien, I am going to stay here, at least for the time being. Now you must excuse me. I must get to the silverware or I shall never complete my task before luncheon."

I went to the storage room behind the pantry in search of the necessary supplies. As I passed by the kitchen I heard Aggie.

"No, Miss Clarissa, not that way. Try this. No, no, miss, that isn't quite it . . . Would you like a nice cup of tea? You've been working so hard."

Clarissa's girlish voice claimed she was exhausted and would love to have tea, and perhaps some honey cakes.

"Now you sit right here, miss. I won't take but a minute."

Wondering how many cups of tea and honey cakes Aggie

could stuff into Clarissa before lunch, I continued on my way, laughing.

I was coming back when I heard Michael's big voice clearing the way. Moving down the hall, wobbling to and fro as it progressed, came a huge chest with two legs. It was a very gay piece of furniture, very brisk and loud as it moved. Briarcliff Manor seemed to be a different kind of place today. I found myself wishing I had not been tucked away to care for the silverware. I longed to be in the main hall or in the parlor with everyone bustling about.

Michael had managed to corrupt the reserved competence of all the servants, and they were now a raucous crew, having as much fun as they were getting work done. I could imagine Miriam's pale eyebrows pulled down low over her prominent eyes as she rushed from one group to the other, trying to encourage the return of our usual decorum.

I was sashaying down the hall, coming as close to a skip as my ailing muscles would allow, when a great arm whipped about my waist, lifting me off my feet and whirling me through the air. I squealed half in pleasure and half in pain as Michael's face nuzzled against my neck. He released me, nearly causing me to fall.

"I'm sorry. I forgot how stiff you must be. Did I hurt you?"

"No," I said. "I'm not that fragile."

"Good!"

Completely recovered from his momentary remorse, he planted a kiss on my cheek and rushed off. Obviously there was no use in telling him he mustn't behave in such a manner in full view of the servants.

Every one of us somehow managed to accomplish out appointed tasks, and the house settled into its normal routine by evening. We had all assembled in the parlor except for Father, who had not yet returned from the city. Michael poured each of the ladies a sherry, and Darien and himself a generous portion of whiskey. It was unlike Father to be late, but no one seemed to be worried.

We were in mid-conversation when the knocker at the front

door sounded. I hated the sound of the knocker. Two, three, four times it rang out, echoing around the high-ceilinged main hall. It did not pause as was normal for a caller, but continued in a slow metronomic rhythm.

We all stopped talking as Jacobs hurried for the door. The knocker was now striking its eighth blow. I could feel the gooseflesh spread along my skin with each successive thud. We were now all on our feet, waiting, when Jacobs' cry of fright brought us *en masse* into the hall.

My father was leaning heavily against the outer wall, his face white and drawn. If I had not known him better, I would have thought him to be insensibly drunk. His arms hung lifelessly at his sides. Only his hands moved, twitching at the ends of his motionless arms.

Miriam rushed to his side and took him with Jacobs' help into the hall. His body slumped to the floor, and she knelt by his side. I stood back, petrified into a solid form incapable of motion or thought. I saw Michael and Darien rush to him, pushing Miriam aside. They repeated the same examination that she had just completed. Then, together, they lifted him. He was a big man, and even Darien and Michael were hard pressed to manage his bulk. Laboriously they made their way across the hall to the stairs. His lifeless arms with the twitching hands attached at the wrist like a manikin's kept slipping from his chest and thudding on the riser of each stair.

Clarissa's piercing scream ran through my spine. Her hands were in tight fists, and the shrill cry kept coming from her open mouth. Miriam shook her roughly, to no effect, while I remained frozen to the spot. Finally Miriam drew her hand and slapped Clarissa hard. Perhaps Miriam, too, had reached the end of her control; she delivered the blow with such force that it knocked them both off balance.

Clarissa reeled, and I jumped to catch her as she staggered toward me.

Miriam glared at me.

"Get her out of here! Get her out!"

Not trusting Miriam for anything, I helped Clarissa toward the kitchen as quickly as possible. My own reaction had set in: I was trembling all over. I turned Clarissa over to Aggie, who immediately took over for me, muttering half to herself and half to soothe Clarissa. Clarissa was sobbing too wildly to care who was with her.

"Oh, mercy, mercy, poor little lamb," said Aggie. "This place ain't fit to live in."

I walked unsteadily out of the kitchen and to the servant's stairs. I heard Miriam sending Ernest for the doctor, and I went up to my father's room.

He had been undressed and placed in bed. He looked like a corpse. I could not help pitying him in spite of my dislike. As a child, I had thought it would please me to see him helpless someday. But now, as I looked at him, I could feel only a deep sadness. I had often read of the peace that comes to the dying, but there was no peace for him. The ugly lines of life still drew his mouth downward as though at any moment his eyes would flicker open and I would see that hateful look he always bestowed on me. But he neither stirred nor opened his eyes.

I walked through his sitting room and into the small study in his suite. I remembered the room well. Before this evening, I had visited it for the first and only time the day he decided to send me away to school, the day he'd had the argument with the stranger that had changed my whole life. I had never found out who that man was, or why he'd had such an affect on our lives.

Now, as I entered the room, I felt only its impersonal masculinity. I sat in my father's deep leather chair, waiting, I suppose, to see if he was going to die. It had grown dark and no one remembered dinner. I doubt if any of us could have eaten any way.

The quiet of Father's room stole over me. I must have dozed off, for when I opened my eyes I heard the doctor's voice coming through the door of the study. It was pitch-dark in the study, but someone had lit candles in the sitting room and I could both see and hear the people there.

Dr. Schwartz was speaking.

"I'm sorry Mrs. Asherton, I can't be more specific. As far as I can tell it was something he ate. I have bled him and we can hope he will be stronger in the next few days. If he hasn't improved by then"—he shrugged his shoulders—"I don't know. He is a very sick man. His breathing is shallow, the paralysis does not seem too bad, but I can give you no further answers without talking to him."

"What good is a doctor? You tell me nothing I can't see for myself—you *do* nothing!"

"I'm sorry, ma'am. We have made great strides in medicine, but we are not sorcerers who can see into the body and mend it by magic. I wish we could give a potion and have a man rise from his bed in good health. I will be back tomorrow. There is nothing to be done for him tonight, so I suggest you get some rest. He will not awaken."

Dr. Schwartz bowed and bade Miriam a good night. Then he turned to say goodbye to someone I could not see. It wasn't until he spoke that I realized it was Michael. Then I heard Darien's voice. They were all in the room except for Clarissa.

I would have made myself known could I have done so without seeming to have deliberately eavesdropped on them. I decided to wait until they had left, and then slip out of the room unnoticed. I heard Darien offer to show the doctor out, and then the sounds of them leaving the room. Miriam turned to gather her shawl from the back of the chair, then blew out the candle that was on the drum table.

The sitting-room door to the hallway shut firmly. I thought it was Michael leaving the room, but I heard his voice.

"Stay where you are, Miriam."

"I'll do no such thing."

He moved swiftly across the room to where she stood, which put them both in my line of vision. I had never before seen this Michael; the look of him frightened me terribly. He took Miriam's arm, and I could see from the expression on her face that his grasp was hurting her. He pushed her down in the chair and stood over her.

"Stay where you are!"

This time she didn't try to move, but remained seated, rubbing at her bruised arm. Nonetheless, her tone was acid when she replied.

120

"Well, what is it, *Cousin* Michael?"

Her eyes met his, and they sparkled with the hate she felt for him.

I pressed my body farther into the leather chair, but was unable to take my eyes from them.

"Don't call me cousin."

"But, my dear, you are my cousin."

"I am no kin of yours, Miriam."

"Well, if you want to be picky . . ." Her tone was almost coy. She was fast regaining her mastery over the situation now that she had managed to divert him from his original train of thought.

"My cousin-in-law is quite good enough."

Michael turned from her and muttered a muffled curse. He was pacing the floor, coming into and going out of my range of vision, when Miriam rose from her chair.

"If that is all you wanted to discuss, I'm afraid I have no time for it."

She began to move toward the door, looking in Michael's direction. I don't believe she was sure of what he might do. He had the look of an animal about him, wary and uncertain. They both moved out of my sight. He must then have taken hold of her again, for I saw her stagger backward into the chair she had just vacated.

For a brief moment she looked frightened.

"Damn you, Miriam! What have you done to him?"

"To whom, Michael?"

She had enunciated each of the three words very clearly, and I wondered where she drew the gall to bait him so.

"Him!"

Michael's hand shot out and pointed toward my father's bedroom door.

"Is it the same stuff you used on my uncle? Don't you think it will look a bit strange, Miriam, if two of your husbands die of the same ailment?"

"But, Michael, dear Michael, you forget, he is not yet my husband. Why would I give him something now? You are over-wrought."

Her tone was impervious, but I sensed Miriam's battle to control her emotions.

Michael paused for a moment before answering.

"I don't know why it should be now," he said finally. "But I know *you*, Miriam. You have an excellent reason for everything you do."

Her eyes flashed at him.

"And what about you? Yes! What about you? What is your game, Michael? Is it not I who should be the accusor? What did you give him? You'd like to see him dead, wouldn't you!"

"What are you talking about?"

Miriam had risen to her feet again, and her voice rose with anger and hate.

"Do you think I am blind? I see you with that simpering Annabel. Do you think I don't know where all John's money goes if he should die before we wed? Do you?"

Miriam took a step forward, and Michael backed away.

"She's a cut below your usual, isn't she, Michael? What has she got for you but money? Did you think I wouldn't notice? Money for everything—is that it, Michael? Michael?"

She kept repeating his name over and over again until I thought I could not stand the sound of it. The malicious rancor of her words swept through me. I had begun to tremble, and I prayed with all my heart that Michael would defend himself in some way. Any way would be enough, if only she didn't say it again.

"Dear God," I prayed, "don't let it be Michael. Please don't let Michael be like George Edgerton."

I clapped my hand over my mouth to keep from crying out. My head was swimming; George's face merging with the angry distorted face I could still see through the open door.

Michael stood still, looking as though he would kill Miriam, but saying nothing, denying nothing.

Miriam slowly and confidently picked up her shawl. A vicious smirk was on her lips. She began to parade herself in front of him, moving in close, her hips undulating as she kept her eyes fixed on his face.

"You hate me, don't you!" Her voice was heavily sweet as she slipped the shawl over her shoulders. "But remember this,

122

Michael. There is nothing you can do. Each of us set a trap for the other, but this time I have you coming and going. John will live, I will marry him, I will get the money, and maybe, just maybe, I'll be able to keep your hands off your uncle's money as well. So don't, Michael—I repeat, don't—interfere with me again. You are the one most in danger. Annabel would believe me if I told her about you—"

"You leave her out of this, and you can also—"

Miriam went right on as though he hadn't spoken. "She wouldn't like it, but she'd have to believe me. So would the authorities, I think. Annabel might not be so cooperative if she thought you were trying to kill her dear father."

He reached out for her again.

"Take your hands off me!"

His hand dropped to his side.

Miriam left the room, not looking back.

I thought Michael would never leave. He kept standing there. I couldn't help looking at him, and I didn't dare show myself. The tears were slowly rolling down my cheeks, dropping onto the silk of my gown. I could barely breathe, and didn't care. Knowing Michael was no better than George made life seem dirty and useless. Clever Michael. Miriam had been right all along. Michael's eyes that had been warm with love only yesterday now burned with the fury of hell itself. His dark hair was mussed, and even knowing what he was, I could feel the strong pull he had for my heart. Why did he have to be as he was? I had called him another George, but I knew he wasn't. I hadn't loved George. I have been a child dreaming dreams, but Michael was different. Now I knew I loved him. I loved him and that made him worse than George, for he had a power over me that George could never have had.

I bowed my head low. I could no longer bear to look at him. I couldn't sit quietly seeing his tall lithe figure, the way he carried his dark head. I remained curled up in the chair, my eyes hidden in my arm for a long time. When the door to the sitting room closed, it shut softly. The sharp little snap of the catch made a sound of finality. Dully I realized I was now free to leave the study that had become my prison.

I moved trancelike down the hall to the other end, where

my rooms were. I fell on the bed fully clothed and slept. My dreams were horrible, crowded with Miriam's venom. My father was a huge balloon being tossed back and forth between Miriam and Michael. Each of them had a long pin, and they fought, shouting at each other to see who would get to burst the balloon. Father's face burst into a million pieces, and they laughed and laughed, and then it would begin over again. Each time, George would pop up like a child's jack-in-the-box.

"I was better, Annabel, I was better."

Around and around they went, each in his turn acting out his grotesquery.

I was exhausted when I awoke the following morning, my face puffy from my miserable night. I slipped into my riding habit, not caring about my aching muscles, not caring about anything; I just wanted to get away.

# 10

THE SUN WAS JUST COMING up when I finished dressing. The room was still a hazy dusk, but I didn't bother to light a candle. I did not want to see myself, and I was certain that I was the only one up and about.

I crept down the hallway like a wraith melting into the shadows. Reaching Father's door, I hesitated only a moment before I turned the knob and let myself into the sitting room. It was airless and stuffy, still smelling of burned candle wax. I glanced to my right and saw the candle I had watched Miriam blow out last night.

I went into his bedroom and stood at the foot of his bed. His position had not changed since last night. I stood there as I had stood so many times at the foot of my mother's bed. As I looked at him, for the first time in my life I attempted to excuse him. I wondered if something had happened to him when he was young to sour him. I knew now how bitter life could be, and I had the persistent feeling that I was gazing upon an image of myself years from now, after I had had time to harden in my bitterness.

I turned from his silent, still form, but did not leave. A wave of pity for him and for myself washed over me. I didn't want to be like my father, but I could feel myself changing, and I didn't know how to stop the process.

If I could have talked to someone—but there was no one in the house I could trust except Clarissa, who was worse than no one in this situation. I wanted to turn to Darien, as I had so many times before, but I could hardly pour out my heart to him—not when Michael was the main subject. I was alone, as I had always been, and that was something I would have to learn to live with as a part of my life. The sooner I accepted it, the better off I would be. Even as I thought it, I knew I was taking the first step toward being like my father, for with my isolation came a certain feeling of strength.

I would be all right if I could just manage to avoid Michael, at least avoid being alone with him. I felt confident of being able to handle myself when the others were around, but I knew I could not yet maintain my firm position if we were alone.

I looked at Father again and touched his forehead. He did not stir, but his forehead was cool, and I knew that must be a good sign. It really didn't matter, I thought. If he lived this time, it would be to fall at the hands of Miriam or Michael another day.

I left the room, closing the door softly behind me and holding my head rigidly as I crossed the sitting room. I would never look in the direction of the study again if I could avoid it. I let myself into the hall and felt relief.

I went quickly down the stairs and through the kitchen into the courtyard that led to the stables.

"Mathew! Matthew!" I called.

He came from the back of the stables. His hair was mussed and rumpled. I didn't think he had been awake for more than a few minutes.

"I thought that was your voice, Miss Annabel. What can I do for— oh, no, miss!"

His eyes were instantly alert.

"You don't mean to take that horse of yours out again?"

"Yes, I do, Matthew. Please saddle Bucephalus now."

Matthew looked uncomfortable.

"I can't do that, miss. Mr. Barington told me you wasn't to ride that horse no more."

"Michael—Mr. Barington—has no right to say what I may or may not do!"

"But, Miss Annabel, you could be killed. That horse ain't fit for you to ride."

My patience snapped. I had taken all the careful concern from Matthew I could tolerate.

"Saddle Bucephalus immediately, Matthew. And I won't hear another word!"

Matthew looked taken aback. I had never before used that tone with him or anyone else.

He took only a few moments to bring Bucephalus to me. He held the horse as I mounted him. As though Bucephalus had joined the forces against me, he began to prance and move about, causing Matthew's face to wrinkle with worry. I had vision of his running for Michael's room the minute I left the stableyard, so I looked down at him and spoke very firmly.

"Matthew, this time under no circumstances are you to go to Mr. Barington. Do you understand?"

"Yes, miss, but supposing something happens?"

"I said under no circumstances, Matthew."

"Yes, miss." He looked pained and unhappy. I couldn't bring myself to leave things as they were. I had hurt his feelings, and had offended his sense of duty to me.

"Matthew," I said more gently, "Ill be all right. I promise I won't jump Bucephalus—not today, anyway."

He gave me a weak smile.

"We can be thankful for that. God be with you, miss."

Bucephalus and I tore across the East Lawn as if pursued by devils. Riding him somehow cleansed my spirit. For these moments we became a part of all things and took from them wholesomeness. My ride, as I told Matthew it would be, was free from incident. It bolstered my confidence to know that I could maintain a normal appearance in front of the others. Bucephalus was behaving more like himself today, and my confidence in him also gave me a lift. Somehow, I would sort out the tangle that had wound itself around my life.

When I gave the horse back to Matthew, his smile this time was sincere. I raced for the house and dashed up the stairs to my room, changing into a suitable dress. By the time I had finished my toilette, it was time for breakfast. I smoothed my hair and went downstairs. Miriam, Darien, and Michael were already there. I flinched at the sight of Michael, but I put a smile on my face and sailed into the room.

"Good morning, everyone."

I stepped to the sideboard and carefully examined the platters of food. Having filled my plate with ham and eggs and cornbread, I turned to Miriam.

"Have you seen my father yet this morning?"

She looked surprised as I took my seat at the table.

"Is he awake?"

I took a bite of ham and chewed it slowly, letting her wait for my reply.

"I don't believe so—at least he wasn't when I was there earlier. I thought you might have seen him since then."

"Why no, the, ah . . . the doctor said there would be no change in him for some time."

She bowed her head, and I could practically hear her brain working as she sought a reasonable excuse for not having seen him. When she looked up she had managed to make her eyes look watery.

"You know, Annabel, it is hard for me to see your father so helpless. A sick room is a place of tragic memories for me. It is a strain I find hard to bear."

"Much like traveling, I imagine."

I knew anyone listening would think me cruel, talking like that, but Miriam vindicated me by a vicious look.

"What do *you* know of grief?"

"Absolutely nothing. I was merely referring to the time you told me that traveling was a trial to you. I thought perhaps visiting my father was similar."

I immediately turned my attention to Darien. I had not been able to so much as look at Michael.

"Darien, do you know when the doctor will be coming?"

"Well, he was here last night. We looked for you to tell you, but you were nowhere to be found."

"No, I'm afraid I fell asleep," I lied. "Will he be returning today?"

"Yes, but not until this afternoon."

"Oh, well, I don't suppose there is much he can do until Father regains consciousness." I carefully put the last bit of my ham into my mouth, looking as innocent as I could when I continued. "After all, doctors are not sorcerers, able to instantly cure, now, are they?"

I saw from the corner of my eye that Michael had brought his head up sharply, looking at me, as was Miriam, with great intensity. I dabbed at my mouth with my napkin.

"If you'll excuse me, please, I have some letters to attend to."

"Annabel!"

Michael's voice called after me, but I did not stop or turn back.

Of course, I had no letters to write, and once I left the room I was at a loss as to what to do with myself. I couldn't let them see me standing there. Time seems longer when you are forced to be alone and idle while others go busily by, full of activity. I went to the greenhouse. It was too warm and humid to be comfortable there, but the warm, fresh smell of the plants was soothing. After the cold strained atmosphere the others created in the house, this was a loving, welcoming place. I touched the long elliptical leaves of an oleander's drooping limb. These, I thought, would accept any gesture offered, and could neither connive nor retaliate.

I got through the day well. I managed to avoid the others except at meals, and to stay away from any conversation with Michael. He looked worried and puzzled, but made no advance toward me. I suppose to him my behavior was an uncomfortable curiosity. Having no way of knowing that I had overheard Miriam and him, he was still under the impression he was succeeding with his plan to win me and Father's money. It always seemed to come down to Father's money.

The doctor arrived just before tea. I happened to see him coming up the front steps to the terrace, so I went to the door myself and accompanied him to my father's room.

Father was awake when Dr. Schwartz and I entered his room—a comical picture for all his irritation. He had slapped his nightcap on his head, and wisps of his coarse hair were sticking out from under it, rather like a porcupine who is not quite sure whether he is under attack or not. Dr. Schwartz was much relieved to see him awake and moving. I left the room and waited in the sitting room while he talked to Father.

I was pleased to note that my nervousness had lessened since this morning. While I still did not want to look at the study, I did not feel unduly uncomfortable. The memories were there, but they were not as forceful as I had thought they might be. When the doctor had finished his examination of my father, I asked him to join me in the sitting room.

"Please sit down," I said to him. He had popped out of his seat when I rose to shut the door to Father's room. Dr. Schwartz nodded his head in approval.

"It is better that he does not hear the other members of the family talking about him. It makes a patient feel there is something he doesn't know about his illness, you know."

I didn't know and I didn't agree, but I said, "Do you know what caused his illness?"

He shook his head.

"It is most puzzling. He has no idea, either. I was certain it was something he had eaten or drunk, but he claims he ate nothing that the rest of the family didn't."

"Do you mean at breakfast?"

I thought for a moment, trying to recall what Father had eaten yesterday morning. We had all taken food from the common serving dishes, except for tea, and Clarissa had had a cup of tea with him.

"What about later in the day?" I asked. "When did he eat lunch?"

"That is the puzzle. He said he had eaten nothing since breakfast. He began to feel ill about lunch time, and did not feel he should eat. He says he started for home immediately."

"But he didn't arrive here until well after eight o'clock."

"He had to stop several times along the way. He is vague about the trip home. He stopped for a while at the farm that adjoins yours on the south, but that is all he seems to be clear about."

"Then if he did not eat in town, which seems doubtful at the moment, it had to be something he ate here."

Dr. Schwartz nodded patiently.

"Could it be anything else?"

"Good heavens, Miss Arbriar, it could be any number of things, but I wouldn't know what."

"That seems very odd to me," I said. "I have never known my father to be ill."

"Well," he said, "that isn't actually the case. He was ill in the same manner about six or seven months ago."

"I wasn't aware of that. What did you feel had caused his illness that time? Was it something he had eaten then as well?"

"I didn't treat him. He was away visiting with friends, and became ill while he was there. When he got home he told me about it. Dr. James, the man who treated him, told him it was caused by a substance toxic to his system."

"He was poisoned!" I gasped at this verification of my worst fears.

But Dr. Schwartz laughed.

"There are many things that can poison a man, Miss Arbriar. They are not always lethal or deliberate."

"But it does mean," I pressed, "that it was a poisonous substance, and not tainted food?"

"Oh, my, yes. Otherwise the rest of you would have been affected."

"Well, I can at least check the kitchens and see what we have around that could be poisonous. You know, we do use poisons in the greenhouse, as well as in the stables."

"You can check through all of those, and if you have a question please feel free to call upon me. When you are dealing with a poison, there is a virtually endless list of substances. If you should happen upon the answer you would be very lucky indeed."

I nodded my head, knowing he was right, and that my chances of finding a handy vial of poison were small indeed. I rose from my seat and so did he, preparing to leave.

"Would you stay for tea, Doctor? We may be a little late, but I'm certain no one will mind under the circumstances."

He agreed to stay and we went downstairs to the front parlor. The weather had turned inclement in the afternoon, and we could not enjoy tea on the terrace. The parlor was a picture of normalcy. Miriam sat before the large silver tea service pouring the pale-green liquid into the delicate china cups. At our approach. she looked up from her task and greeted us cheerfully.

"I didn't know you had come, Dr. Schwartz. Forgive me for not greeting you. I failed to hear the door."

"Miss Arbriar met me as I was arriving. I never knocked on the door, so you have no need for your gracious apologies. I have been well taken care of."

As he spoke, he was eyeing the oven-warm scones and assorted cakes on the tray. Miriam asked him to be seated, and he took a chair next to her.

Clarissa was sitting on a pretty pink satin lady's chair, looking like one of the frosted cakes she was so fond of. She was busily chatting with Darien between tiny bites of her sweet cake.

Michael came up to me, took me to the other lady's chair, and pulled one of the straight-backed chairs up close to it for himself. There was little I could do without creating a scene.

"Thank you, Michael," I said shortly.

"Is your father better this afternoon?"

"Yes, much better. But it is still a matter of considerable time, I fear, before he is himself."

"Is that what has been worrying you?"

Like a gift he had handed me the perfect excuse for my changed behavior, but I was too preoccupied with containing my emotions in his presence to take advantage of it.

"No!" I said, clipping off the end of the word as it dawned on me that I had just lost a golden opportunity. "My father will be all right. I'm sure of that.

"What makes you so sure?"

I began to form an answer, but saw he wasn't looking at me. Dr. Schwartz had his full attention, and I could see him strain to overhear the doctor's words to Miriam. Dr. Schwartz rose from his seat and made his goodbyes, promising to come again tomorrow to see my father.

132

Michael was on his feet, and had not even noticed that I had failed to answer him.

Perversely, I felt disappointed that I had managed to escape Michael's grasp so easily. I watched him talk to Dr. Schwartz and then walk toward the door with him. He did not so much as glance in my direction.

Miriam half rose from her seat as though she might follow the men into the hall. She glanced about and noticed Clarissa and me looking at her. She sat down again and gave a little self-conscious giggle.

"I guess Michael can manage to see Dr. Schwartz out by himself."

Clarissa sighed. "I would think so," she said in a bored tone. "Anyone could. We do not always need your constant supervision, Miriam."

Clarissa's voice trailed off, and she rose from her seat. She did not look to see what, if any, effect her words had had on Miriam, but left the room.

Minutes later the parlor was empty except for me, and I sat wondering what Michael had wanted to see Dr. Schwartz about. I was certain, after my conversation with the doctor, that my father's illness was no accident; but what could Michael possible want to know from him? If Miriam had spoken the truth last night, Michael must already know all there was to know about Father's ailment. As always when I tried to sort out the threads of Miriam's and Michael's lives, I would up in tangles and knots.

I gave up and went for a walk in the garden. It was raining lightly, so I soon returned to the house. It was becoming more and more difficult to keep my distance from the rest of the people there.

# 11

THERE WAS LITTLE FOR any of us to do, for with Father incapacitated, the wedding plans were very much up in the air. He was improving rapidly; the difference in his condition could be seen in one day. He was pleased with his progress, but while he showed no permanent damage, he was exceedingly weak and tired quickly.

On the third day it became apparent that something had to be done about the wedding. It was already late to be changing plans, but Father, by sheer force of temper and strength of voice—neither of which had been affected by his illness—had stubbornly refused to change the date of the wedding or any of the planned festivities. Even Miriam seemed at a loss in dealing with him. I, better than most, knew how loath she would be to put off the wedding, but she tried. Eventually she was forced to turn to me for aid. I willingly obliged, for I would have postponed the wedding permanently if I could.

If it turned out to be Michael who wished Father dead, he would gain nothing if he did not have me as his wife, and I would see that he did not. On the other hand, if it was Miriam who wished Father dead, she needed him as a husband. The idea of a postponement gave me much relief and some time to plan.

On the morning that Miriam asked me to help her with Father, we were just finishing breakfast. Clarissa with her usual childish frankness asked Miriam about her predicament.

"What will you do, Miriam? I just can't fathom how you will manage all those people . . . just hundreds of people all over the house, and John not able to stay awake for a full hour at a time."

Miriam didn't answer her, but Clarissa quickly became carried away with the scene she was imagining.

"Can't you just see us all gathered for the ceremony, and right at the moment John is to take his vow to you he will fall fast asleep."

She giggled, and choked her words. "And . . . and we will all have to adjourn until he awakens to complete the ceremony."

All of us were chuckling—all but Miriam, who was very distressed. I do believe the imaginary happening was as real to her as it was to Clarissa.

"Clarissa, please! Will you stop this nonsense. It is no laughing matter."

She turned to me.

"Annabel, I don't know what to do. John is being impossible. Will you see if you can help me convince him that we must postpone the wedding?"

I knew then how real her distress was, for she had spoken in front of the others. For her to request my help at all was unusual; for her to do it with the others present was downright startling.

"I can try," I said. "But you know what effect my suggestions usually have on Father."

"Oh, yes, I do know, but something must be done, it simply must. I'm willing to try anything. He can't stand the strain of the reception we have planned. People will say I am dragging him to the altar."

"It would be uncomfortable to have people thinking such thoughts . . . I would imagine."

The sarcasm in my tone was lost on Miriam, for she looked up at me with as sincere as expression as it was possible for Miriam to have.

"It would indeed. I don't understand John. How can anyone be so muleheaded? And so oblivious to what people would say. Surely he can see what a position he would be placing me in."

Her exasperation seemed genuine enough, and I wondered why she hadn't been aware of my father's selfishness and his stubborn traits sooner. She was at a loss, for once, and I found her more natural and likable this way. Even her selfish and petty motives had a refreshing ring of truth.

"When would you like for us to talk to Father?"

"Let's go now. If only he will listen."

Father was awake. Jacobs, who had brought him his breakfast, was paying for his kindness.

"It's no wonder I'm sick!" The sound of my father's voice came to us as we walked down the hall. "This isn't fit for the dogs."

We entered the room as he flicked his eggs off the tray.

"It's cold! I'm on my deathbed, and you can't manage one good meal. Miriam! Send that Varka boy up here to help me."

He started to get out of bed, his skinny legs dangling out from his nightshirt.

"Father!" I cried. "Get back into your bed. Miriam and I are in the room."

"Of course you're in the room, you damned idiot. Think I've gone blind too? You're my daughter, and she'll be my wife tomorrow. It's high time both of you knew what a man looks like."

Once more he began to get out of bed, taking care to shock us. I caught my breath and blushed. I had never heard or seen him behave this badly before.

Jacobs did not even excuse himself, but scooped up the egg and rushed out the door, lest he become entangled in what promised to be an even more embarrassing scene.

"Father, please! We can't talk to you like this, and we must speak to you. It is a matter of utmost importance. Please get back under the covers."

He muttered under his breath and looked warily at Miriam, who was nodding frantically. Grudgingly he began to settle back into bed, more from the strain of exertion, I think, than from any desire to accommodate Miriam or me.

Beside me Miriam took a deep breath and moved closer to his bedside. I followed her.

"Father," I said, "something must be done about the wedding tomorrow. People are coming from all around. Some will be arriving this very afternoon if we don't stop them, and you cannot stand the strain of a long day such as you have planned. They must be told. It may be too late even now to get a message to some of those who live at a distance."

"This is none of your affair, Annabel. Who asked you to interfere?"

"Miriam did," I said. "You are being completely unreasonable, and seem determined to make fools out of both of you."

He laughed harshly. "Fools, you say! You are telling me that I would be making fools out of Miriam and myself? You, the queen of fools?"

"I don't deny that, Father. It only serves to make me a more knowledgeable judge of what I am telling you. How do you think you would look if you collapsed during the ceremony? Or perhaps it will be in the midst of the party afterward that you collapse. It'll be a pretty figure you'd cut, sprawled unconscious on the floor. Wouldn't it?"

Miriam's eyes rolled upward in real dread of the possibility.

"I do think you should at least talk with Miriam about it. You would not look very dignified, I can tell you that."

I did not wait for a reply but left the room, thinking Miriam could better deal with him from this point on. I knew Father would seriously consider his appearance before an audience.

Miriam came to me later. As soon as I saw her, I knew she had been successful. Her air of discomposure had vanished, to be replaced by her usual look of smug self-assurance.

"Annabel, your father has finally agreed to compromise. It was very shrewd of you to play upon his pride as you did."

I smiled, feeling warm inside at my private victory over her.

"I am glad I could help you, Miriam. For how long did you decide to postpone the wedding?"

"Oh, we didn't."

I tried hard not to show my disappointment.

"But I thought you just said—"

She laughed lightly. "Your father came up with a much better plan. We will be married as planned tomorrow, but it will be a small, intimate wedding, just the family. And we will postpone the wedding banquet indefinitely. And, of course, there is no question of a wedding trip; that too will be put off for the time being. All of the problems are solved, and as John says, we will be married on schedule."

I felt a great emptiness in my stomach. This was a possibility I should have considered. Father's pride was a double-edged sword. He would not appear foolish in front of people, but neither would he submit to any alteration of his own desires.

I forced sincerity into my voice when I spoke again.

"That is a very agreeable arrangement for you. You must be pleased."

She nodded agreement, but the expression on her face told me she had not yet come to her purpose for having sought me out this second time.

"I have already sent Jacobs, Ernest, Matthews, Peters"—she counted off all the male servants on her fingers—"to cancel the invitations and offer apologies and explanations. However, I must ask your assistance once more."

"What would you have me do?"

"I must go to town and cancel many of the orders we have made. If it is not done immediately they will be delivered this very afternoon, but I also have an appointment with the dressmaker—my wedding gown. I cannot do both. Would you go to town for me?"

"Of course. I'd enjoy the ride, and I have some shopping to do myself."

"That's fine; it will work out well for both of us." She paused for a moment. "Michael will have to drive you. I best go find him."

"Oh, Miriam, don't bother Michael. I can manage perfectly well by myself. Really."

"Well, if you're sure . . ."

"*Who* is not to bother me?"

I don't know where Michael came from. I sometimes suspected him of the ability to walk through walls. He simply appeared.

"Oh, it's nothing, Michael. Annabel is going into town for me, and I thought she might want someone to drive for her, but it turns out I was wrong."

"Not at all. I shall be delighted to drive. When do you want to leave?"

I could think of no graceful way out of this situation.

"I must leave very soon, as the orders are due shortly. It will be too inconvenient for you, I'm sure."

"An hour?" he asked.

"Thank you, Michael, but I must be there before they have started out for the house. I really don't want to inconvenience you."

"Michael, stop worrying her. She has already said she will drive herself. Obviously she would prefer it that way."

Michael did not glance at Miriam. He fixed his gaze on me.

"I'll be waiting for you whenever you are ready to leave."

"It will take me about half an hour," I said.

"I'll have your carriage waiting, ma'am." He bowed to me, triumphant, and left the room.

He was waiting near the front door when I came down the stairs. As I saw him standing in the hall with arms folded across his chest, his head crooked slightly to one side as he watched me descend the stairs, the horrors of the other night seemed very far away indeed.

But the hard reality was that I must keep that night in mind every instant I was with Michael. One day, someday, I would be able to forget him. He would be leaving after the wedding, and that would make it easier for me.

I had not brought a shawl with me, and Michael advised me to return for one, as it was turning colder. We got on our way later than planned. I was afraid I would be too late to prevent the extra food being delivered, but Michael had no such concern. He let the horses jog along at a leisurely pace, and he seemed determined to notice every leaf on every tree we passed. I was forever underestimating him, and I now know he was deliberately annoying me so that I would reach the point where my temper would master my tongue, forcing me to say what was on my mind.

"Michael, will you please hurry. I will not get there in time if we continue at this pace."

He did nothing to hurry the horses.

"Why have you been avoiding me for the last two days, Annabel? What have I done to annoy you?"

"I have not been avoiding you. And you are annoying me *now,* by allowing these horses to crawl into town."

His tone changed.

"Don't be so flippant with me, Annabel. It doesn't become you. Something has happened to change you. You behave as if we were strangers."

"We very nearly are, you know. I've known you only a little over a week."

He brought the horses to the side of the road and halted them. He turned to me, took me roughly by the shoulders, and forced me to face him.

"I love you," he said. "And I thought you loved me, but something has changed you. What was it?"

I didn't answer.

"Something did happen, didn't it?"

Again I didn't answer.

"The night your father became ill, that was the night."

I bowed my head and remained silent. He said nothing nor moved for a moment. Then he put his hand beneath my chin, raising my face so that his eyes looked intently into mine.

"Where were you that night?"

I tried to look away, but he held my chin firmly in place.

"Where *were* you? Answer me, Annabel!"

"In Father's study," I whispered.

"Oh, my God! You didn't . . ."

I nodded.

"But you couldn't have *believed* her!"

I hadn't any power left in me to nod or deny. The hateful

141

tears slipped down my face, and I was helpless before him. I could not trust him, but neither could I resist him as he pulled me close, rocking me to and fro like a lost child. He whispered gently, softly through my hair.

"Don't, Annabel, don't. I could never harm you. Never . . ."

I felt myself giving way, being absorbed by him, by the warmth of his body as he held me close against him, hearing his heart as it beat steadily and strong beneath my ear.

He loosened his grip on me so he could see my face.

"I love you, Annabel. With all my heart I love you. Can't you believe that?"

I could not stop the flow of tears, and his words did nothing to aid me. Seeing him as he was now, gentle and unhappy, and hearing his voice tell me the things I had longed to hear such a short time ago was more than I could stand. I thought my heart would burst.

"I don't know, Michael." I sobbed. "I want to believe you. I want you to . . . but Miriam said all those things, and you—"

"How can you listen to that woman? Don't you realize what she is?"

I straightened myself up again, and finally stopped crying.

"She is your cousin," I said. "And you came here with her. Why? You must have had a reason. I don't believe you wanted to chaperon her, or to be a member of her wedding party."

"She is not my cousin. She married my uncle. I suppose that makes us cousins of a sort."

He was looking at some distant point, and I longed to know his thoughts. His face was a study of concentration. The only evidence of the soft and gentle Michael of moments before was his hair. The independent and unruly locks had found their way in waves about his forehead. They did not belong to this serious and disturbed man, but to the Michael I dreamed of and loved.

"She is an evil woman," he said. "I know she murdered my uncle, and I think she has the same end in mind for your father."

He was still gazing before him, talking as much to himself as to me.

142

"Uncle Charles was very much like your father, not quite so wealthy, but rich enough to attract Miriam. They were married less than a year when he suddenly took ill. He died of a mysterious malady. His stomach, the doctor said, but it was the same as your father's illness, only in his case it was fatal."

"Is that what you spoke to the doctor about yesterday?"

"Yes."

"Then why are you with Miriam, if you suspect her of being a murderess?"

He turned to me, and his eyes were deep pools in which I might drown.

"I started out with two reasons, but now I have only one."

I sat rigidly in my seat, refusing to respond to him.

He gave in to my determination and continued.

"Uncle Charles accidentally outsmarted Miriam. He wrote a new will when they were married. I had been the principal heir before that, but he wrote a new one naming Miriam as his heir, and put it away. The will has never been found. No one knows who drew it up, for he did not go to his own lawyers. Mr. Bishop, Uncle Charles's lawyer, disapproved of the marriage and they parted ways. We do not even know who wrote the new will for him."

He paused for a moment, looking at me as though he were trying to make up his mind about something.

"Miriam thinks I have made off with it."

"Did you?"

"No."

"Then you are the heir?"

"Someday I will be. She has managed to hold up Uncle Charles's estate in the courts. She will never win in the end, but she has been able to prevent me from settling it. When she knew she was going to marry your father, she intimated that if I would assist her, she would release her hold on the property."

He paused again. I knew he was trying to gauge my reactions to what he was telling me.

"What did she want you to do? How could you assist her?"

He didn't speak for a moment, but kept looking at me. I was beginning to feel uncomfortable when he took a deep breath.

"She wanted me to convince you to leave here. I was to . . . bring you into my sphere of influence . . . so you would listen to me, or, if necessary, so you would come away with me if I asked you to. It wasn't as bad as it sounds, Annabel. I didn't know you, but I would have been happy to get anyone away from Miriam's influence. When I found out what she wanted of me, I knew she was not merely interested in marrying your father. There was more to it than that. She would not have needed you out of the way if she was sincere about wanting a family as she claimed. So I agreed to do as she asked."

He stopped talking, and was looking intently at the reins in his hand.

"You said you had two reasons. That is only one."

I wanted him to go, knowing, as I now did, the foundation for Miriam's threat to him. If only he could rid me of the rest of my fears.

"The other was Miriam herself. I have no proof that she killed Uncle Charles, but I'm certain she did. We've never been able to discover what she used to kill him. If I could just identify what it was, I would have her."

"Couldn't the doctor help you with that?"

"He tried for a while. There were so many things it could have been, and to be honest, he wasn't sure that I wasn't accusing Miriam of something for my own gain."

"He might well think that, I suppose. You did have as much to gain as Miriam."

He did not reply, and I wondered if the same thought had come to his mind that had come into mine. There was no question that he and Miriam were once again in similar circumstances, each of them having a great deal to gain from the death of another person.

"After the doctor had given up, what did you do?"

"There wasn't much I could do. I stayed as close to her as I could. She did nothing out of the ordinary for some time, and then about seven months ago she met your father. She was a houseguest at the Logans', and so was John. Darien and your father have done business with Mr. Logan for several years now, and often stay at his house when they are in town.

144

"John became quite ill that weekend. I grew interested when I heard it was caused by something he had eaten, and that Miriam had stayed on to nurse him herself. I thought I could stop her if I accompanied her here—and, perhaps, gain the evidence I needed to prove the murder of Uncle Charles."

He stopped for a moment. I knew he was no longer explaining to me, but trying to answer a question he had himself. I waited quietly and he continued in a thoughtful manner.

"What I don't understand is why she let me come with her to Briarcliff Manor in the first place. She even asked me to. She knows what I'm trying to do; she must have a reason for wanting me here."

He was very absorbed in his own thinking. I kept my expression serious to match his own, but my heart was smiling when I prodded him.

"And what is your one reason now?"

"What?" he asked distractedly.

"You said you have only one reason now. What is it?"

His change of expression was comical as he realized he had won.

"You are a minx!"

He pulled me toward him and kissed me enthusiastically. Then he pushed me away from him, looking carefully into my face to see if I really meant it. His eyes softened, lighting from within me a warmth that played tricks with my breathing. He drew me close against him as his mouth sought mine. I put my arms about his neck in the most unladylike fashion and returned his kisses with my own.

It was some time before we continued on our way—I no longer cared if I got to town on time or not.

There were still questions: Why would Miriam, if it had been Miriam, poison my father before the wedding?

Michael said he did not have the answers. For the time being, I was content to revel in my feeling of having come home once more, and for me "home" meant Michael. I could obtain no proof that what he told me was true, but it no longer mattered.

We arrived at the shopkeeper's just in time—the cart was

being loaded as we drove up. We hadn't the nerve to cancel the order completely, so we amended it to foodstuffs and supplies that we could use in the ordinary course of living. The shop-keeper seemed content with the new order.

I did my shopping while Michael, who had gone off with a spring to his walk and warmed me, waited at the tavern for me. I made short shrift of my errands, and was again by his side within an hour.

We talked happily of the future on the ride back. Only once did he return to our earlier subject.

"Annabel, you don't want to leave Briarcliff Manor, do you?"

"No, I don't. Nor do I feel I *can* leave as things now stand."

"I thought that was what you would say. I won't try to dissuade you, but I am worried about it."

"Why?"

"You have no place in Miriam's plans. I don't know what she might do."

"Do you mean to *me?*"

"Just be careful. I still don't like that accident you had with Bucephalus."

"Did you find something out about that? Something you haven't told me?"

"I don't know if I found anything out or not. Matthew told me Darien had taken that horse out every day for the two weeks before you came home. It seemed odd to me, but I don't know if it means anything or not. The horse doesn't like him, but that seems to be all."

I thought of what he said, but had nothing to add. I had also thought Bucephalus' behavior around Darien strange, but I could not account for it in any way.

"If anything peculiar should happen, Annabel, come to me right away. Will you?"

"Yes, of course."

His next question surprised me.

"Do you know Darien well?"

I wondered how to answer. I had been around Darien off and on throughout my life. We were friends, and I had only

146

recently been very attracted to him. But when I thought about it, I hardly knew the man.

"No," I said. "I don't think so. But he is an excellent horseman, and I don't understand why Bucephalus behaved that way with him if he had been riding the horse every day for two weeks."

Michael dropped the subject, and we spoke no more of the troubled affairs of Briarcliff.

Once I had been deposited at the front door, I hurried off in search of Miriam. I reported faithfully that I had accomplished my task, and she needn't worry. She hardly noticed me, just went busily off in her own direction as soon as I finished speaking.

As I spoke to her, I had tried to see her as a murderess, but could see only the same disagreeable woman I had met when I first arrived. And when I tried to envision the reality of what Michael had said, it seemed fantastic and impossible.

# 12

THE NEXT DAY, MY father's wedding day, was clear and cool. He and Miriam were to be married at one o'clock in the afternoon. We spent most of the morning scurrying about arranging things to suit our altered plans.

Clarissa and I dressed in the gowns Miriam had selected for us. She had chosen well. They were most becoming, though more daring in cut than I would have chosen. Clarissa's gown was like Clarissa herself, pink and rose and covered with laces and frills. Given the opportunity, Clarissa would have selected just such a gown.

And I would have selected mine. It was made of satin, in the softest shade of blue. The bodice was cut low and framed in ivory lace of the same type as that which formed a panel on the front of the skirt. It had none of the frills or flounces I disliked, but fit tightly across my bosom and waist, flowing gently into a full graceful skirt. I looked at myself approvingly, hoping that Michael would be as pleased with my appearance as I was.

Clarissa and I came down the stairs together. Darien and Michael were awaiting us. No one had designated how we were to pair off, and I had blithely assumed I would be Michael's partner. But now I noticed Darien looking at me as though he expected I would be with him. And that was the way we went into the parlor. I cannot say how disappointed I was.

Father did not, as Clarissa had predicted, fall asleep while pledging himself to Miriam. We all played our roles successfully, and my father and Miriam were married in the third week of September 1867 without event.

I had expected something to happen. It always seems as though some powerful spirit should make known the truth when a wrong is being done. But nothing happened, and none of those present indicated in any way that this marriage was anything other than what it appeared to be.

I now had a stepmother. Both she and my father looked pleased and happy. We all gathered around, congratulating them. My father promptly took advantage of the occasion to kiss Clarissa soundly. Michael came to stand beside me, and we stood watching them silently, apart from the others.

There was some commotion as Jacobs entered the room, followed by Aggie and Bertha bearing champagne and trays of food. They were dressed up in their best uniforms for the occasion, and had taken special pains to make the trays of food attractive and decorative. It was difficult to think of the terrible things that might happen when everyone was making a special effort to be cheerful, so we all forgot our wariness of one another and joined in the celebration.

Before long it became obvious that Father was tiring. Miriam persuaded him to go to his rooms. We all promised to come up to see him later. After telling us to enjoy ourselves, he turned to Jacobs and ordered him to fetch more champagne for us, and to bring some to Miriam and himself in his sitting room.

The four of us who remained in the room seemed to lose our joyful spirit as soon as the necessity for it was gone. We raised our glasses and made the customary toasts to the newly married couple, and then our voices faded away, with an uncomfortable silence.

Although we all seemed to like one another individually, it was not possible for us to get along well as a group. Clarissa had tired of her flirtations with Michael, and Darien did not respond to her, so she was bored and took no pains to hide it.

Darien and Michael in their best days had little to say to one another, and now had virtually nothing. We made the best of things for a reasonable length of time, and then each of us went off in his or her own direction.

In the days that followed, the house sluggishly settled into its new routine. Miriam took over complete control of the house, and I found that I didn't mind helping her learn the few details of its management she did not already know. I even talked Aggie into staying on as cook, for a trial period, of course, but with Aggie that was as good as a promise.

The biggest change was in Miriam's attitude toward me. She appeared to be making every effort to be friendly. There were no more tricks, and she stopped trying to convince me I should leave. I wondered whether she had told other people that I was going to travel while she assured me it was no longer a necessity. I could not forget Peggy's conversation with Edith and me the night of the ball at the Hites'. It had annoyed me at the time that Miriam would be so presumptuous. Now in the face of her friendliness, rather than being reassured I felt all the more hesitant.

I did not let my thoughts come to the fore, however. I knew it was better to hope and work to make the three of us as normal a family as possible, whatever doubts remained in the back of my mind.

Miriam talked happily of plans she had for spring parties, to be given primarily in my honor. In spite of the fact that I was rather old for the sort of plans she had, I did not question her but listened with interest as she spoke of the young men I would meet. Nor did I say anything about the relationship that was developing between Michael and me, for she seemed to have no inkling of it, and Michael had made it clear that he did not feel it necessary or desirable for the others to know.

Michael had become a sore point with Miriam—in fact the only one observable these days.

"I don't understand why he continues to stay on," she said one day. "He was planning to leave as soon as the wedding was over, and now he seems to be settling in."

That had been her first comment, but it was not her last. She continued to fret about Michael's presence. As for Clarissa, she was anxious to leave and did not care for the idea of traveling alone. She had been waiting patiently for Michael ever since the wedding, but now she was more than ready to take her leave of the quiet atmosphere at Briarcliff Manor.

One day, about a month after the wedding, Miriam and I were in the morning room. She was planning the week's menu, and I was writing a long overdue letter.

Neither of us saw Michael on the terrace, but he must have seen me, for he entered through the terrace doors and came over toward me. I could read his intention in the expression on his face, so I indicated to him by gesture the presence of Miriam before he embarrassed us both. As he stopped and turned to greet her with exaggerated cheer, I had to smile. He was such an incorrigible creature. When he chose to act upon impulse, heaven only knew where it would lead.

This time it led to a disquieting reaction in Miriam. For the first time since her marriage I saw a terrible, harsh expression cross her face. Perhaps because of its absence I was unprepared, the look of her frightened me as it never had before. before.

"What *do* you want, Michael?"

I could see immediately that this scene would turn nasty indeed if Michael decided to confront her. I did not really understand either of them. I had allowed myself to be lulled by the peaceful quiet of Briarcliff Manor in the last month, and I was not prepared for it to shatter. I had also had Michael's never-failing attentions to me. But he had not said a word about us to the others, that was obvious, and I could not very well go about telling them we were in love if he were unwilling to have it known. I had thought it would ease the problem of his staying on at Briarcliff Manor, but he did not agree, so I had drifted along, gradually losing my apprehension and fear.

Now they stood before one another, adversaries once more. How strange, I thought. I was Miriam who wanted him here in the first place to win me over; why was she now equally determined to be rid of him, and to keep me at Briarcliff Manor?

Perhaps Michael had been wrong, and she wanted him only as a witness to her wedding. Or perhaps he had been right, but we had entered into a part of her planning that even Michael had not suspected.

Whatever the case, I did not like it, and could never feel comfortable when the two of them were together. Michael was like a stranger to me when he was around Miriam. I was too aware of the underlying tensions between them, and they frightened me.

Michael stood before her now, proud and cynical.

"Since you ask," he said, "I want to speak with Annabel."

"Annabel is busy, as you can see."

I began to protest, but she continued, looking up and deliberately stopping me from speaking.

"I'm quite sure she has too much to do the entire morning to be able to while away any time with you."

Michael's eyebrows raised quizzically, and I knew in that instant he would not leave quietly.

"Well, Miriam, you are being quite the protective step-mother this morning, aren't you?"

She considered him for a moment and said, "Perhaps so. It may be as you say. And as her stepmother I feel that I must tell you that your extended presence here is very unseemly."

"Unseemly or inconvenient?"

"Both!"

The edges of her eyes began to redden as they always did when she was trying to control her anger.

"But either reason is sufficient for me to demand that you end your visit, Michael. You are no longer needed here, and your presence is not wanted."

Her voice was rising, and I calmed my impulse to intervene. I had frequently been driven to confront Miriam, but I was too much the coward to come between her and Michael. To watch them was frightening: they seemed pitted against one another in a deadly war. And so I sat rigid on my chair, holding tightly to the sides as their hostility filled the room.

"Don't trouble me with your reasons, Miriam. I am not leaving."

Her hand clenched, crumpling the menu she had been working on.

"You shall!"

Her eyes seemed to start from her head, as they had done the night Father had become ill. I could not help myself; I began to shake with nervousness as the memories of that night closed in on me. Miriam's voice was so loud and shrill, and her anger so intense, that I felt as though the walls were coming in on me, as though I were once more trapped in the darkness as I had been that other night.

I wanted to leave the room. I wanted to get away from her—and from Michael. Yet I could see no escape that would not draw their attention to me, so I remained in my seat.

Now she was shouting at him, her loathing totally unconcealed.

"You shall! You shall leave here. This is my house! Do you hear? Mine! You have no right to defy me."

"I have every right in the world," Michael replied, his voice cold and controlled. "Don't threaten me and don't order me, Miriam."

Suddenly she calmed down. I could not follow her sudden and inexplicable shifts of mood and temper. She now spoke as quietly as though she had never been upset, yet so slowly that the effect was more terrible than the shouting had been.

"You will be out of this house by noon on Thursday or . . . I . . . will . . . have . . . you . . . put . . . out . . . bodily!"

"Will you, now? By whom? Jacobs is rather old for that kind of activity. Your husband? Who, Miriam? Or will it be your lackey—Darien?"

"My lackey?" she seemed amused. "It might be."

She smiled and looked at him intently. "I would like to see that. You and Darien." Her eyes roved over his body. "You would make a good match."

Michael looked disgusted. He started to speak, then turned on his heel and left.

Miriam looked over at me, speaking as though she had just returned from a dull afternoon of talk.

"He is a most tiring man. I should never have asked him here."

I couldn't answer her. As quickly as I could, I pretended to finish my correspondence and left the room.

The relief I felt after walking out was almost tangible. I raced up the stairs, changed into my riding habit, and went immediately to the stables. I tried not to let anyone notice that I was upset. I only wanted to ride until I could rid myself of the feeling that had come over me in the morning room.

Bucephalus had become much more his old self in the last month. While I had not attempted to jump him again, I was no longer afraid to ride him.

I did not stop for my usual banter with Matthew, but rode away on Bucephalus as quickly as I could. We crossed the East Lawn and went into the hemlocks. I was pleased when he started toward the path leading to the jump, for I felt it was a sign he was losing his fear. I let him follow it until he came to the curve, and then I reined him in and dismounted. There was a nice open grassy patch just off the path. Bucephalus happily nibbled at the choice little clover blossoms, and I sat against one of the hemlocks.

I kept seeing before me the expression of Miriam's face as she raced through the moods that came and went so fleetingly with her. The total unpredictability of her rage made me apprehensive and nervous.

I wondered what Michael would do. Today was Tuesday. Would he leave? I didn't believe Miriam would actually have put him out, as she had threatened. No sane person could possibly want such a controntation between the two men. But it still didn't leave much of a choice. If Michael remained, it was sure to be unpleasant, and if he left . . . what if he left with *me*?

I got up and went to Bucephalus. I hurried back to the house, giddy with the prospect of running away with Michael. Surely I could see him alone, later in the day.

I did not see Michael that day, or in the evening, or all day on Wednesday. He seemed to have dropped out of sight. By Wednesday afternoon I was almost convinced that he had left without so much as a goodbye. Edgy and unhappy, I put all my pride and my upbringing in my pocket and crept cautiously up the back staircase. My heard pounded wildly as I stole into Michael's room.

I closed the door quickly behind me, and raced to the

wardrobe. I hesitated just for a moment, afraid to see the empty drawers before me. The opened easily. I laughed out loud with joy and relief. There they were! His shirts were all neatly stacked. I opened another drawer, irrationally convinced that he had left without his shirts. But his jewel box, handkerchiefs, men's things smelling of fresh laundry soap and leather were all in place. At least I knew he hadn't left, but I had no more idea of where he might be now than before. I hurriedly closed the wardrobe and stole from the room.

I tripped lightly down the stairs. Someone must have seen him. I went first to Aggie. She said he had taken the few meals he had eaten in the kitchen, but she did not know where he was now. I went from person to person but no one knew Michael's whereabouts. Matthew was my last hope.

"No, miss, I haven't seen Mr. Barington since early this morning."

"Well, when did you see him this morning?"

"Oh, it was early, miss. He come here to get the carriage. I haven't seen him since."

Matthew stood patiently awaiting more questions, but I remained silent.

"When he returns, should I tell him you are looking for him, miss?"

I thought not. In spite of the disappointment Matthew would feel at my refusal to allow him to play matchmaker, I was certain he would tell Michael anyway.

"No, Matthew, I'll undoubtedly see him myself later."

"Yes, miss."

But I did not see him later. I dressed carefully for dinner, feeling certain he would be there. Darien met me at the foot of the stairs. During the past month he and I had been able to reestablish our earlier easygoing friendship, and I no longer felt the hesitation I had felt that night in the summerhouse.

As I now looked at him, I could see only the handsome man I had seen when I first returned. I had thought of him often recently, and had wished it had been him that I loved rather than Michael. He was always there. He remained calm, strong, reassuring. It was true that he could not stir me as Michael did, but I did not feel I could stand much more of the tension I had experienced recently. One could never be certain of anything where Michael was concerned.

Uncertainty had taken its toll of me, and now, as I went down to dinner, I quite frankly didn't know what I should do if Michael did not appear.

Darien reached out to me, taking my hand firmly in his own.

"You look lovely," he said, his eyes light in appreciation. "Tonight I shall have you to myself for once."

He took my arm and led me into the library. Father was looking himself once again. Miriam sat near him.

"Good evening, Annabel. Come and join us in a toast. We have cause for celebration tonight."

I looked closely at Miriam as she spoke. She looked more vivacious tonight than I had ever seen her. She had an air about her I could not define, almost a quality of excitement.

"What are we celebrating?" I asked, looking about the room as though Michael might pop out of the woodwork if I stared hard enough. But there were only Clarissa, Miriam, my father, Darien, and I.

Realizing my attention had wandered, I listed carefully as Father spoke.

"The doctor has given me a clean bill of health."

He looked over at Miriam and gave a gruff little laugh.

"Tomorrow I am to be let out of my cage for a while."

Miriam looked up at him and patted him on the knee.

"Not for too long at first, John. You must promise me you will remember to take things slowly." Then she turned her attention to me. "We have planned a nice little outing. Will you join us? It would please your father and me."

"Yes, of course." I could hardly refuse under the circumstances. "I would like that. Where are we to go?"

Darien replied for the others.

"It is just a trip around Briarcliff Manor. Nothing really. We are going to the old guesthouse in the south field."

"That old ruin? Why, it is all crumbling and falling down."

As I spoke, Darien smiled sheepishly.

"Well, this outing is really to be a combination of business and pleasure. I must go there to check on the condition of the walls and one of the chimneys. One of the men told me several of them are no longer safe."

"I see," I said, not seeing at all.

"We thought we would take advantage of the ride out and back," Miriam added. "It is beautiful, except for the old house." She smiled and squeezed Father's hand.

Clarissa interrupted this tender scene to announce news of her own.

"Well, I too have a celebration."

She lifted her empty glass, which Darien refilled, and then he filled the rest. Clarissa waited patiently until he had finished.

"I am going back to civilization again. Tomorrow!"

I had to smile, she was so obviously pleased and happy at the prospect.

"What time of day will you leave, Clarissa?" I asked her.

"Early tomorrow morning. Michael says we must leave here no later than ten o'clock."

"Michael?"

"Oh, yes," said Miriam. "We are finally to be rid of Michael. Don't you recall, Annabel, that Michael had planned to leave this Thursday?"

I looked stupidly at her.

"Yes . . . yes, of course, I remember now. You and Michael are leaving together, Clarissa? Tomorrow?"

"Yes. Isn't it wonderful?"

"It's wonderful for you. It is just that I will miss you."

"Why don't you come with us?"

Darien immediately moved closer to me and put his arm around my shoulder possessively.

"We will see to it that she isn't lonely."

I was amazed at Darien's move toward me. He had never acted this way before, not even when I thought there might be something between us. Since then I had not given Darien a thought in that way. Michael kept me in such a state of confusion, and the atmosphere in the house had become so unpleasant, that I had simply counted on Darien as a good friend.

158

I had a sickly feeling that I had made a bad error in judgment. I did not want to hurt him, and I knew there was no chance I would love him. Michael had destroyed any hope I might have had of loving anyone else. Even now, leaving as he was, without so much as a word, I could only love him.

Miriam's voice broke into my thoughts.

"Will you be ready to go with us by noon, Annabel?"

"Yes," I said. "I'll be ready."

"Good. We will leave soon after Clarissa and Michael go."

# 13

WE WENT IN TO DINNER, where the talk was all of Clarissa's plans for the future.

As dessert was being served, Darien leaned over close to me.

"Meet me on the terrace, Annabel. I want to speak to you."

He had spoken so softly that I nodded my assent rather than speaking. My father glanced over at us, but said nothing. I had no idea why Darien felt a need for secrecy, but obviously he did. All through the meal I had been expecting Michael to make one of his sudden appearances, but he hadn't. His place was set at the table, to my right.

I was feeling very tense and jumpy. I would be glad to get outside, and I didn't think I could stand one more moment of talk. I was growing irritable; each reply I was forced to make was becoming more difficult and trying.

I excused myself from the others, saying I had a headache. Darien had already disappeared, making no excuse whatever, and his manner had made it clear that he had a destination. I knew it would look most peculiar and deliberate if I too disappeared into the night. So I stood in the doorway and made some inane comment or other, and again referred to my headache.

My father raised his eyebrows.

"I hope you recover quickly," he said.

That was as close to humor as Father ever got, so I gave him a slight smile and thanked him for his concern.

The air was chilly, and I went upstairs to get a shawl. Darien was already on the terrace, pacing back and forth, when I arrived. He looked nervous and intent. I pulled my shawl close against the wind and went to him.

"There you are," he said. "I thought you weren't coming."

"I had to make some excuse for not going to the parlor with the others . . . and I had to get my shawl."

His face lost some of its tension.

"Of course," he said. "I should have realized that."

He shook his head as though trying to clear it. When he looked at me again, his expression was happy, almost excited.

"Do you remember what I told you in the summerhouse?"

"You told me several things that night."

"Yes, but I mean about wanting to get away sometimes, and that some things seem to be determined before the people involved are aware of them."

"Yes, I remember that. At the time, I thought it was unlike you."

"It isn't, though. It is something I have thought about and known since I was a little child. Some things just have to happen a certain way."

He stopped speaking and looked down at the slate of the terrace.

"What is it you wanted to say, Darien?"

I pulled my shawl closer to me again. I did not know if it was the cold wind or the tension from my day of searching for Michael, but I had begun to shiver and was very uncomfortable. I was trying to think of a tactful way to go back inside without appearing to dismiss him as unimportant, when he spoke.

"Come away from here. Leave. Tonight."

His words hung in the air like little darts. I could not believe what I heard—Darien, standing before me saying the words I should be hearing from Michael's lips. All night long I had sat tense and unhappy till my head really did ache, and my neck strained with the effort of merely supporting my head, and now I had fallen into some cockeyed dream where all the people and the events were scrambled.

"Leave . . . but where . . . have . . . I can't leave, Darien! . . . Where would I go?"

"With me. We'll go together, just as it was meant to be."

My heart was beating too hard and too fast. I did not know what to say or do; my reactions were sluggish as the full meaning of his words came to me. Certainly I was not prepared to handle such a situation as this tonight, of all nights.

"With you? Now?"

I am sure that I was no more able to control the expression on my face than I had controlled my words. Each time I opened my mouth something more revealing came out of it. I was making things worse by the moment, and I could not seem to help myself. There was no doubt that he now understood that what he felt to be preordained, I had never even thought of, at least not in the way he meant.

I had never seen Darien angry before. He had always been agreeable, and pleasant. Even when I had been so disappointed in him that night in the summerhouse—the same night, it seemed, that he became sure of our destinies in the exact opposite way from what I had concluded—I still held to my image of him with the sun in his hair as I saw him on my first day home.

Now, in the dark, with the anger in his eyes, I knew what Edith had meant. All the beauty of his handsome face froze into a mask, incredibly ugly. Suddenly it was as if all my fears and suspicions of the last month came together to be caught up in Darien's face, and I was unreasonably frightened.

"Yes, with me!" he was saying. I felt he was far away, but he was actually standing very close to me. "What did you think? It is Michael who has ruined you."

"Michael has nothing to do with this. I didn't know you had this in mind, that you cared for me this way. I thought we were just friends."

"I have seen you with him . . . going off behind my back."

I moved several steps away from him. His lips were drawn back so that in the dark it looked as though he were smiling, but I knew he wasn't.

"Behind your *back?* Darien! You don't own me. I didn't know, I never went behind your back. We've never—"

"No, *we've* never," he said, taking me roughly by the shoulders, "but *you* have. Trying to act innocent won't help you now, Annabel."

I tried to pull away from him. His grip on me was like iron.

"I'm not!" I cried out.

"Are you coming with me, Annabel? I'll forget all the rest."

He did not relax his grip, and I did not know what to say to him. If I answered him truthfully I didn't know what he would do, and I was terrified by the sudden change in him. But I was even less sure of what he would do if I lied and agreed to do anything he said. I might be able to get away to the safety of my room, but as he was now, I might as likely be thrust into a carriage and taken off into the night to God only knew where or what.

Oh, Michael! I called inside my head. Where are you now that I need you?

I had exhausted Darien's patience with my silence. He shook me harshly.

"Well?" he demanded. "Are you coming or not?"

"No."

I closed my eyes, dreading whatever might come.

"No?" Amazingly, his voice held disbelief. "Fool. You don't know what you have done. Fool!"

He spat the word at me and thrust me away. I backed into the terrace wall, and he turned hastily, bumping against me as he ran down the steps and out into the lawn.

I stood there in the cold night, my teeth chattering as I listened to his retreating feet.

I thought of our trip tomorrow, and became frightened all over again. Somehow I would refuse to go. No! I wouldn't. I was afraid to be left in the house alone. At least if I went I would be with Father and Miriam. Surely there was nothing Darien could do with them along.

I suddenly wanted to get away from Briarcliff Manor as fast as I could. I tried to calm myself—here I had just told Darien I didn't want to leave, and in the next moment had wished desperately to be gone.

I ran to my room, not caring how confused I was. I pulled out my writing paper, and as soon as I could control the pen I began to write to Sue Ellen. To her and to any other friend whose name came into my mind, to all those I had just left last summer, I wrote that I was returning to Europe. Some I told England, and others I told I would be returning to France. With no pride whatsoever, I asked if I might pay each of them a visit. I would write to them later of my arrival date.

When I looked over the letters I had written, I could barely recognize my own handwriting. It was a scrawl, the hand of a woman not in her right mind. I kept writing as though my life depended on it.

I paid particular attention to the letter for Sue Ellen. She would be the only one who could possibly understand my fear. I should have listened to her, so many years ago, when she told me never to come back to Briarcliff Manor. She hadn't wanted me to come this last time, either. So I wrote her letter over and over, trying to make it sound normal, or as normal as the kind of tale I had to tell could sound. I don't recall going to bed. I suppose I did, once I had used up all my paper. I know that I did go to bed only because I awoke there the next morning. My clothes were scattered about the room.

For the briefest of moments I could not think what had happened. I was normally a neat person. I saw the letters lying on the floor or covering the desk, and I remembered the whole situation. Then, with a start, I thought of Michael's departure. I had to see him. I looked wildly at the clock on my mantel, knowing it was late. Nine thirty.

"Thanks be!" I said to the empty room. I still had time. I ignored the disorder of my room, grabbed the first dress my hand touched, and put it on. It happened to be the rose dress I had worn the day Darien took me to see the Briarcliff Manor grounds. I hadn't worn it since. Had I not been afraid of missing Michael, I would have changed it.

I tore down the stairs. There were no sounds in the house. I wasted precious minutes running from room to room. Lettie saw me as I rushed back down the hallway.

"Whatever has happened, Miss Annabel? What is wrong?"

"Nothing," I said irritably. "Where *is* everyone?"

Her concern at my behavior was evident in the tone of her voice as she answered me.

"Why, they are all outside, miss. Mr. Barington and Miss Clarissa are taking their leave."

I left at a headlong run for the front door.

I burst among the small group assembled there like a madwoman. I realized what I must look like, and I could feel my face going hot and red as I stood there trying to regain my breath. Michael was there, looking perfectly normal.

"Are you in a hurry, Annabel?" he said as if he had never disappeared. Had I been carrying an umbrella I would have crowned him with it. He was such an infuriating man.

"Is something wrong?" asked Clarissa, for once sensible, now that I could not be.

"No," I said, still breathing hard. "I overslept, and I thought I had missed you. I ran down the stairs, that's all."

I was still gasping for breath, and everyone stood waiting as though I would say something else.

"I wanted to say goodbye."

I shot a hateful glance at Michael, which he returned with a grin.

As I went over to Clarissa, kissing her on the cheek, he said, "Well, you made it. And I appreciate your caring."

He took my hand as though it belonged to someone he had met, for the first time, earlier that day.

"I thank you for your kindness and hospitality."

"Michael!" My voice was dangerously high.

"Goodbye, Annabel."

He kissed me lightly on the cheek. I wished I could shoo the others away. I had to talk to him, at least know where he was going, if he would write, come back, something. He couldn't just leave like this, like a guest, a stranger.

166

"Michael . . ." I began.

Father moved quickly, his big voice cutting across my high-pitched hysteria.

"Annabel! Get hold of yourself. You are behaving very badly. What in the devil has come over you?"

He took hold of me as though I were a recalcitrant child and began pushing me into the house. I closed my mouth and pulled at him to stop dragging me away. He looked warily at me, but released his hold. I looked to Clarissa. I said goodbye to her again, and she agreed to write to me. I turned to face Michael. His eyes were full of unspoken words, but I could not tell what they were. He mounted the step of the carriage. Moments later, he was gone.

I stood there miserably staring at the spot where the carriage had stood.

"Annabel," said Father, "whatever is wrong with you? You had better rest . . . see the doctor. Do something to get hold of yourself."

Miriam came immediately to where we stood.

"John, don't be like that. Annabel explained—she overslept and just isn't fully awake yet. Isn't that so, dear?"

As she spoke she smoothed a lock of my hair which had fallen out of place. Father made a rumbling sound in his throat as I stood like a stuffed doll between them.

"You see?" Miriam said sweetly. "That is all that is wrong. You must learn not to upset yourself like this, John. She will be just fine on our drive. I want both of you to remember, this is a special day, the day of our celebration." She looked around her, and pointed out that we were not wearing coats.

"Even the weather has turned in our favor. The drive will do wonders for both of you."

She seemed to have settled the matter for all of us, and we moved dutifully toward the door.

"Shall we get ready to leave now?" she asked. "We can get an earlier start than we thought."

She seemed in very high spirits indeed, happier than I had ever seen her. And well she should have been—everything had happened as she wished. She was married, she had Briarcliff Manor, I was obedient to her wishes, if unwilling, and Michael was gone.

I went upstairs and tried to straighten myself out. My hair was like a rat's nest. I had shoved it atop my head when I awoke, and now it was drooping and falling from loosely placed pins. I looked at my disheveled face in the mirror, and wondered at my calm.

"Why aren't you crying? Don't you know what has happened to you?" I asked my image. I did not cry. I didn't seem to have any tears, or any feelings at all. As distraught as I had been earlier, the girl who looked out at me from the mirror was now totally calm. I fixed my hair and straightened my dress as though this were a day made unusual only by the prospect of a pleasant drive in the country.

I was the first to arrive downstairs. Darien was just coming through the front door. I no longer felt the fear I had last night, but I did not want to be alone with him. I thought too that he might dislike me now.

Nor could I blame him as much for his behavior now as I had last night. After all, I had just finished making a spectacle of myself in front of everyone. I had been as violent in my own way as Darien had been last night. I knew now that I had managed *that* situation very badly. I expected him to resent it, but he looked his normal self. His face was alight with a smile, and he came forward immediately to greet me.

"Good day, Annabel." His look was as admiring as it had been on that other day I had worn this dress. "You look beautiful."

As I looked at him I thought, I do not understand men. I loved Michael, I would have run barefoot to the ends of the world for him, and he left. I was a friend to Darien, and he wanted to run away with me. There was no sense to it.

Darien was not the fearsome creature I had imagined last night. He was simply a man who had mistaken friendship for something greater, and if I were honest he had had some reason for thinking it. I would take my cue from him. Perhaps someday I too would recover from my disappointment over

Michael. Darien and I were not dissimilar in our problems this morning. He was cheerful; well, so would I be.

We walked out on the front terrace. The sun was very warm in spite of the brisk air. It was not necessary to wear a coat or even a shawl. We talked easily as we waited for Miriam and my father.

"Well," said my father when the finally emerged from the house. "You look as though you have regained your wits."

Darien looked concerned.

"Did something happen this morning?"

"No," I said. "I was just in an awful rush, as I was late in getting up. It upset Father." And to my father I said, "I am quite recovered now, Father. You see. I am very much myself."

"Everything is just as I said, John," said Miriam. "There was no need for you to get yourself in a state over Annabel. Now, let's be on our way."

Lightly, gracefully, she led the way down the steps and toward the carriage.

# 14

FATHER AND MIRIAM SAT in the rear of the open carriage, and I sat in the front with Darien. Father and Miriam were talking happily in the back. For the first few minutes I strained to hear their conversation, but it was nearly impossible.

Seeing my efforts, Darien shrugged his shoulders and smiled as though in apology.

"I'm afraid you might as well give up. It is one of the disadvantages of this carriage . . . or advantages, if you prefer to have private conversations."

At that moment Miriam leaned forward in her seat.

"Are you comfortable up there, Annabel?"

"Yes," I called back to her. "We are just fine."

Darien looked over at me and smiled. "I hear we lost our houseguests this morning."

"They left about an hour ago."

He laughed.

"I was beginning to think they were planning on settling in for the winter."

"It did seem as though they might. You sound as though you are glad to see them go."

171

He shrugged his shoulders. "Not really. I don't care one way or the other."

I did not want to pursue the subject any further, for fear it would jolt me out of my numbness.

Dreading the moment I would again be able to think and to feel, I changed the subject.

"Why was the house we will visit allowed to fall into disrepair?"

For a moment he just looked at me in surprise.

"I don't suppose you do know anything about that house," he said finally. "Do you?"

"No, I know nothing of it. I have never even seen it. Matthew told me not to go there because it was a complete ruin and very dangerous."

"It is a ruin, but not really dangerous unless you plan trying to climb on it, or disturb it."

"How did it become as it is?"

"I burned it," he said flatly.

"What?" I was sure I had not misunderstood him.

"I burned it . . . But don't look so alarmed. I had a perfect right. It had been my home, and I burned it to the ground."

I tried to keep my voice in check, lest Father think I was having another spell. I glanced at him, but he was engrossed by whatever it was Miriam was saying.

"Does Father know you burned the house?"

Darien's expression was one of complete peace, very much at odds with the turn our conversation was taking.

"Not fully. He knows it was burned, but he does not know it was I who burned it."

"Why *did* you?"

"I just told you. It was my home. I could do with it as I liked."

"But, Darien, it was a *guesthouse*."

He laughed, and I did not like the sound of it.

"It was never a guesthouse. It belonged to my father, and then to me. In a way, all of Briarcliff Manor belongs to me."

"Darien!"

"You know so little, Annabel. Haven't you ever talked to your father about this place?"

172

"No."

"You should have."

"Then why don't you tell me now? You seem to know a great deal about it."

He looked at me appraisingly.

"All right," he said. "I will. You have a right to know."

His eyes crinkled at the sides as he squinted, as though trying to decide where to begin his story of Briarcliff Manor, the imaginary Briarcliff Manor, I thought, that belonged to him. I was very curious as to how he would explain his claim on my home.

"About thirty-five years ago, your father and mine came out here, each one looking for land. I'm not certain how they met—it isn't important—but they did meet. Their ambitions were very much the same, and they eventually became partners. Neither of them was a poor man, but neither of them had enough money to buy and develop the land that later became Briarcliff Manor. So they pooled their resources and—"

"They bought the property *together?*"

He nodded.

"Then this story you are telling me is true?"

"Of course. What did you think?"

"I don't know. When you said in a way you owned Briarcliff Manor, I thought you were going to tell me some story of being underpaid for your years of work, or that Father would not recognize your value, or something."

"I could tell you those stories, too," he said, smiling. "But the story I am telling you now is also true, and it how Briarcliff Manor came into existence. They bought the land together, but because your father had put in the greater amount of money, he was first to choose which section of the land he wanted."

He stopped talking.

"What are you thinking about now, Darien?" I finally asked him.

He looked over at me, smiling.

"Nothing much. I was just wondering how far ahead John was able to see when he made his choice of the land."

"Well, what happened? Why did your father leave?"

"He didn't leave. He is buried not far from the house."

"Oh, I'm sorry, Darien. I didn't think when I said that. I knew your father was dead, I just didn't know that it had happened here."

"It's all right. He is where he would want to be. Your mother is buried by his side, you know."

"My mother? Why? She's supposed to be in the mausoleum. How—"

"You don't know *any* of this do you? I am sorry. I wish you had come with me last night."

I barely noticed his mention of last night. What he was saying couldn't be true. How could I have lived here all this time, and not known any of this? It was a fantastic story he was making up—to impress me, or frighten me.

I looked at his strong profile, and I remembered his tone when he told me it was true, and I believed him.

"Please finish."

"Are you sure you want to hear all of it?"

"I'm sure."

He settled back in his seat.

"Where was I . . . oh, the land choice. Well, your father chose the part where the Manor now stands. His area was bordered by the brook, the one you jump with Bucephalus. That was the east boundary, and part of the south where it curves. Now, do you know where the Hudson runs to the north?"

I nodded.

"That is the north boundary. And the most important one, for the river was the most important source of water that kept both farms producing, regardless of weather. In the dry spells, the little brook was used to carry water from the river. When we diverted the water, all the south fields could be kept in good condition. My father's share of the land lies south of the brook, and out of reach of the river. John controlled all of the water that mattered as far as irrigation was concerned."

I was afraid of the direction this seemed to be taking, and I asked my next question with more hope than conviction.

"But if they both had access to the brook there was no problem, was there?"

174

"No," he said. "Not as long as the water was diverted into the brook."

"Wasn't it?"

"At first, yes. But things changed, soon after I was born."

"What did you have to do with anything?" I asked unthinkingly.

He smiled again.

"Nothing, directly. You know your father wanted a son. Your mother had not had any children when I was born, and John felt that he was being passed by. So when I was born he tried to make the best of his feelings, but he was jealous of my father. Then my mother died as a result of childbirth."

"I'm sorry, Darien. This must not be an easy story for you to tell. If you would rather not, I understand."

"No, I think you should know it all. My mother's death could not be helped, and it was probably best after all. My father was at a loss as to what to do with me. So your mother sent a girl down from Briarcliff Manor to care for me. And Grace, your mother, was a warm, loving woman, and she came every day to be certain all was as it should be.

"She and my father became friends. He said that was all it was then, but your father was a very jealous man. He forbade her to come near Varka property, and she obeyed him. During that time, you were born, and your father was again disappointed that you were not a boy.

"When I was about eight—you must have been two—I became very ill. It had been a bad winter and spring, and I had caught a fever. Your mother came back to help my father. Both she and my father nursed me until I was well again. During that time they fell in love."

"My mother and your father?"

I could imagine my father's wrath if he had even suspected, let alone known this to be true.

"Did Father know?"

"Oh, yes. He knew. He came up on them one day. I remember it well. I was recovering, but still in bed. They had come in to check on me and had thought I was asleep.

"Grace and Papa went into the herb garden at the side of the house. From my window I could see them. I watched for a long time. They fascinated me, and made me feel good. They were gentle and loving with one another. You are quite like she was then," he said, looking at me. "That is what appealed to me most when you came home. I had never noticed it before."

"I think you are mistaken," I said. "My mother was known to be quite beautiful."

"She was, and so are you. Didn't you know that is why your father dislikes you so?"

I flushed.

"No, Darien, I didn't. I don't think I ever thought much about it. I never knew Father to act any other way toward me, so I never questioned it."

"Well, it is so. That and not having a son."

He had stopped talking again, and I waited patiently for him to go on until I could stand it no more.

"Well, what happened that day . . . as you were watching them?"

His voice came as though from some far-off place.

"They were sitting on a bench, much like the one you prefer in the dogwood garden, and they were in each other's arms . . ."

His breathing was shallow, and the expression on his face was one of pain and fear. I knew he was seeing that moment all over again, and I held my breath as I listened.

"They kissed one another, paying no attention to anything around them. Your father came up. I saw him from a distance, riding a great black stallion he had then. He looked like the devil from hell coming upon them. His hair was raven black, and he was dressed all in black astride the huge black stallion. He was raging. I could see from my window. They didn't hear the horse, and I rapped on my window, shouting, 'Papa!' trying to warn them.

"They didn't hear me either. It was too late, even then, but I kept on trying. I got out of bed, but when I tried to stand up my head spun and I fell back. I managed to crawl outside just as John struck Papa on the side of the head. He came up on that horse, crowding in, and brought the crop down against my

176

father. Papa fell and struck his head on the bench. Your mother was screaming. John dismounted and came toward her. She thought Papa was dead, and so did I—there was a bloody gash near his temple, where he had struck the bench. The blood kept trickling down.

"Grace lunged at your father, crying and beating at him with her fists. He stood still, letting her flail away at him until she was exhausted, and then he struck her again and again until she crumpled at his feet. He got on that horse and rode away, leaving them there together on the ground.

"It took me a long time to reach them. I kept falling down, and everything was spinning, but I got there. I tried to awaken Grace, first. I was afraid to touch Papa. I thought he was dead. I shook Grace and patted at her bruised face. I pleaded and cried, trying to make her hear me. I kept thinking of Papa, but I couldn't go near him. But he got up, with the blood flowing down the side of his head. He fell to his knees beside us, and he took Grace and me in his arms. I saw my father cry for her. I had never seen a man cry before. I don't think at that time I had even seen a woman cry—we had been happy.

"Neither of us could awaken her. When he was able, Papa carried her into the house. The doctor came, but he could do nothing for her, either. I don't know who it was—the doctor, I suppose—who went to John and told him of Grace's condition, and how it looked having her at our house. John ordered the doctor to bring her back to Briarcliff Manor. He wouldn't come for her himself. When John became insistent, Papa and I, for I was now on my feet again, took her back to Briarcliff Manor. That was the last time Papa ever saw her. John would not let him near her room. She never got well. She had been badly bruised, but she was nearly recovered from those before we took her back to Briarcliff Manor. Something else in her just never healed. If he could just have seen her, one more time—he tried, God, for years he tried, but John wouldn't let him near her."

He stopped talking, and for a long while I could not bring myself to say anything. I felt sick. I looked back at my father, and remembered the man who had come to talk to my father, had begged my father to see my mother. I had thought that man had ruined my life, because that was when my father had sent me away to Miss Hamilton's.

I kept looking at Father and Miriam together. Sick and ashamed, I wondered at the cruelty of him. All these years he had said nothing . . . watched her die, hated her, hated me. After a while I could look at Darien again.

"Why did you stay?" I asked him.

"I had to."

He said it as though it was the most logical thing in the world.

"I don't see how you could stand the sight of him. I can hardly look at him now."

"I hate him, Annabel. But don't you see, he is evil. He must pay for what he has done."

"But how can you make him pay?"

"Oh, I can . . . now. For a long time I didn't know what to do. But I had to keep trying to find a way. I was the only one left who knew what he had done. So today he has a large debt that has come due."

"What do you mean?"

"I mean he has two lives to pay for. Two deaths."

"Another?"

"Yes, you forget my father."

"I know he harmed your father in the cruelest of manners, but you can't blame him for his death. He didn't kill him . . . did he?"

"It was because of him that my father died, and that we lost the land."

I hoped he would continue without my asking. I wanted to know the rest, however painful it might be.

"Remember what I told you about the water on Briarcliff Manor?"

"Yes, I remember."

"Well, about a year after this happened we had a dry spell. My father went to yours, as they had agreed years before. He didn't want to go, but he had no choice. John refused to divert the water. They had terrible rows about it, but John would not give in."

178

"I remember Father arguing with a man who came often to Briarcliff Manor. I am sure from what you have told me that it was your father."

"It probably was. John hated Papa, and they could not even greet each other on the street without showing animosity. After John had refused and Papa knew there was no way to change his mind, he told me we'd have to wait it through. It couldn't last forever, he said. But for us it did. More and more of the land lay fallow. It was uncultivated and barren. When the dry spell broke, it was too late. It would have taken too much time and money to get it back into operation.

"In order to keep us going at all, Papa began to sell the land piece by piece. John offered to buy it, of course, but my father refused. He said he would rather give it away than sell it to John. So he sold it wherever he could, at a much lower price. But no matter what he did, your father always managed to have it in the end. There seemed to be no way of stopping him. Finally we had only the property that the house stood on. There wasn't enough land to do any real farming, and we couldn't count on having enough water even if we did attempt it."

He paused again for a moment. I didn't say anything to him about it, but bit by bit I was remembering the conversation Darien's father had had with mine, and I knew that Darien was telling me the truth. He now looked so sad as I watched him that I wondered how I could have ever seen him as a man who walked in sunshine. Behind his laughing eyes and easy manner had lain this whole sordid story of my father's deliberate destruction of the man who had been his partner.

Darien sighed deeply as if it were a great trial to go on, and his voice sounded tired when he resumed speaking.

"There was nothing to do. So Papa left me to do the little farming we did, and he went to work as a laborer in town. He felt guilty, for he had planned to send me to school, but as it was there was no hope of it. He kept saying one day things would be different.

"One night when Papa was very late in returning home, a knock sounded at the door. We never kept it locked, so I knew it was a stranger or someone who did not have the freedom of our house. It was your father. I had hated the sight of him ever since your mother had died.

"He came in and looked about the house. Then he sat in a chair by the fire, and took a cigar from his pocket. He bit off the tip and spat it on the floor, then told me—just *told* me—'Your father is dead.' He looked at me with no expression whatsoever on his face and then added, 'You'd better go fetch him.'

"I didn't know whether to believe him or not, so I asked him what happened. He said Papa had been killed in a duel over a woman. I didn't believe him, and told him so. I asked who the duel was with. He said he didn't know.

"He started to leave, but he turned at the door. He spat another piece of tobacco on the floor and took a deep puff on the cigar. 'If you want him, he's lying in a ditch by the side of the road,' he said. Then he left.

"I went out to see if he had been telling the truth. It didn't seem possible, but it was. My father lay just as he said. There was a bullet wound in his head."

"It *wasn't* Father, was it?" My voice shook as I asked the terrible question. I could still hear the sound of his voice as he screamed at the man in the hall: "If I ever see you here again, I'll shoot you. I'll leave your damned body in the ditch to rot . . ." Had my father actually gone out and shot this man?

"Was it Father, Darien?" I repeated.

"I don't know. It was no duel, but whether my father died by his own hand or your father's doesn't really matter. Either way, John killed him."

I bowed my head.

"Oh, Darien, it's all so awful. I don't know what to say, there *are* no words."

"No," he said. "There are no words."

Somehow, he managed to smile at me.

"Words never solve our sorrows, do they, Annabel?"

"No," I said. "I don't suppose they do, but somehow they are comforting."

"Not in the end, they're not. Deeds are what count."

He was looking in the distance. I followed his gaze and saw that the house was in sight—Darien's house. I realized that this was the place where my mother had actually died, that she had never really been alive those years she lay in her bed at Briarcliff Manor. In a way she had been more his mother than mine, for *I* had never known her.

Darien seemed in no hurry to get to the house; he just held the horses to their slow leisurely pace.

"This is your house," I said from deep within my thoughts.

"It isn't any more. I traded it away."

This seemed to please him, and he looked over at me.

"About a year after my father died, I knew I'd have to do something, and the land was no good to me as it was, so I went to your father. I knew that originally John and Papa had agreed to take care of each other's families in the event that one of them should die. I didn't expect him to honor the agreement, but I thought I would remind him of it, and use the remainder of the land as an added temptation. I knew he would never be satisfied until he had all of it.

"I had also decided I would threaten to spread the whole story about my father and John all over the county if I had to. Your father is a proud man, Annabel, and I was sure he would respond to that if nothing else worked. But I never had to mention it. He said he would help me for a price."

"The land," I said.

He nodded. "I went away to school, and then returned here. That was also part of the agreement . . . that I work for him and manage Briarcliff Manor until you married, or he found someone suitable to take over. You were at school when we made the agreement, and I was at school when you came back here." He laughed suddenly. "I never thought of that before, but I wonder if John was making certain I wouldn't be here when you were being sought after by all the eligible young men."

"He wouldn't have done that, I don't think. I'm certain he would have been pleased if I had married you. He would have had his son, *and* someone capable of running Briarcliff Manor."

His eyebrows raised. "And, in the end, turn Briarcliff Manor over to a Varka?"

"I hadn't thought of that. No, he wouldn't. It would have been a kind of justice, though."

"It could have been . . . if you had only come with me last

night. We wouldn't have come to this day if you had. Miriam could have gone her way, and I mine—with you."

"Darien, I'm sure you are aware of why I couldn't go with you."

"Michael."

"Yes," I said. "But what did you say about Miriam? You once told me you didn't know her well."

"I don't really. No one ever knows a madwoman well."

"What do you mean?"

"I met Miriam when I was at school, and I have seen her many times since at the Logans'."

"Logan?" The name sounded familiar, but I couldn't place it. "Do I know them?"

"I don't think so. They are business associates of John's. He met Miriam there."

"Oh," I said remembering. "When he became ill the first time, he was visiting the Logans."

"That was the first time she poisoned him."

I whirled in my seat toward Miriam, horrified. Miriam looked up at me smiling. She said something, but I could not understand all the words. Whatever it was, Father joined in and his big voice boomed over the wind and the noise.

"Darien! Turn this thing back. You'll have to come out here by yourself later."

I did not know why Father wanted to turn back. Perhaps he did not want to come to this place again. I couldn't blame him after what he had done, or perhaps he was just tired and wanted to rest. Darien shouted back to him that we were almost there, and we continued to jog along in the same direction. Miriam was leaning close to my father, talking rapidly, probably trying to convince him the trip back would be more tiring if we did not stop first for a rest. He seemed to be quieting and settling back into his seat. I returned my attention to Darien.

"You said the first time."

"What?"

"The first time she poisoned him. Why did she do it?"

182

"It was very simple, really. I had told her about him, and she wanted his money. She killed her other husbands, you know. One turned out to be worthless, and Michael spoiled the other for her. She was a bit hasty with her plans, and Michael made off with a will. They are still wrangling with each other over that."

Then Michael had been right. His uncle Charles had been murdered by Miriam.

"But I don't understand why she poisoned Father *then?* They weren't married. What had she to gain?"

"No, but she had to get to know him. She is an attractive woman, and she took a chance. She thought if she could nurse him back to health she could win him. It worked."

"Yes, I see that it did. But what about that time at Briarcliff Manor? That was poison, too, wasn't it?"

He nodded.

"Did Miriam do that? Or was it Michael?" I asked with a lump in my throat.

Darien turned quickly to face me.

"Did you really think it was Michael?"

"Miriam said it was Michael. I didn't want to believe it, but she had a good reason for her story. She didn't seem to have anything to gain, while Michael . . . could have."

Darien looked at me all the time I spoke, as though he were just realizing something.

"Miriam is counting on that reasoning. She hopes everyone will look toward Michael when your father dies. And if they do, they will conclude he killed his uncle in the same manner. Michael has been breathing down Miriam's neck ever since Charles Asherton died. This is the first time she has been able to maneuver him into a position where she could get rid of him."

"Then everything Michael told me is true! But it is worse, much worse than he imagined . . . I am glad he left. At least now he can't be accused of something he didn't do."

Darien laughed. It was not a kind laugh.

"Why are you laughing?"

He didn't answer me, and I was angry.

"How can you sit there after all you have told me, and make light of her trying to blame an innocent man of murder? He would be hanged."

He did not sound remorseful when he said, "I am sorry, Annabel. I forget your tender feelings for Michael."

"My feelings have nothing to do with it! I don't understand your attitude at all, Darien. You of all people should want to stop her."

"Don't worry about that! I will stop Miriam. She will never have Briarcliff Manor."

"Briarcliff Manor!" I sputtered. "What about the people? What about her husbands, and my father and Michael? Four men?"

"There are some things you cannot stop, Annabel. Miriam and Michael . . . and your father, too, are beyond you now."

His words left me without a reply. I was certain Darien was telling the truth, but I could not help but feel there was more to come, and that in some twisted way neither my father nor Michael was out of Miriam's influence. I tried to collect my thoughts. I could hear the murmur of Father's and Miriam's voices, their words being whipped away by the wind. I wondered if their conversations had had the same macabre undertones that ours had.

Darien brought the horses to a halt, and we stood before the wreckage of what had been his home. It was large and built of stone gathered from the land, just as Briarcliff Manor itself had been. Parts of it still stood, but others had crumbled to the ground. What I supposed had been the parlor still gave the appearance of a room, perhaps one at its beginning rather than its end. The kitchen had suffered the ravages of fire and time the most. It was barely identifiable: most of the outer wall had caved in, and the others looked as though they were held only by the webs of the spiders that lived in them. I shuddered. The sight only added to the apprehension I felt about the rest of Darien's life.

Father and Miriam had gotten out of the carriage as soon as it had stopped. Father was grumbling and complaining about

184

the day. He was hungry, he said, and Miriam had spirited him away from the house without lunch.

"I should never have married you," he bellowed at her. "No woman is worth having. You're all stupid."

Miriam turned back to the carriage, and took from it a large wicker basket.

"John," she said, "I have not spirited you away without any lunch. You see?" She held out the basket she had just taken from the carriage.

Darien moved from my side and was going toward the back of the carriage as I watched my father, who had been responsible for my mother's death, and probably Darien's father's, being soothed by Miriam, herself thoughtfully planning *his* death. As I sat there, a helpless observer, I heard Darien calling.

"I'll just be a moment, Annabel. I have to get the tools out."

I nodded to him, thinking how strangely normal we all were. Miriam was spreading a picnic cloth on the ground. My father was rummaging through the picnic basket, taking the choicest tidbits for himself.

I suddenly turned toward Darien.

"Darien, let's leave here. Take us back to Briarcliff Manor now."

"I can't do that. I have to get that chimney down. See how it's leaning? It's dangerous as it is."

"Please," I said. "I want to get away from Miriam. I can't stand to watch them."

"Come down, Annabel," he said, holding his hands out to help me down from the carriage.

"Come have lunch. You'll feel better then. I have upset you. I should never have told you all this. It seemed, at the time, that you should know."

His voice trailed off as he spoke, and mine sounded loud in contrast.

"Eat! How can you even think of food? Why do you want to stay around Miriam?"

He did not answer, but took me by the hand and began to walk. I thought he was taking me over to Miriam and Father, but he passed them and only stopped to say we were not hungry and would go for a walk. We came to a copse of trees on ground slightly higher than the house.

I knew immediately that he was taking me to my mother's grave. It was a thoughtful thing to do, and so like the Darien I thought I had known. Calming down, I thanked him. He stood beside me, his face peaceful, and I knew he came here often.

These two people buried at my feet represented all that he had ever known of goodness and love, and my father had destroyed them both. I could no longer wonder at his anger last night on the terrace. It made so much more sense to me now. I must have appeared to destroy love, just as my father had. I could understand how he could resent Michael and me. He put his hands on either side of my cheeks.

"I'll leave you here, Annabel. Come down when you are ready. There is no need to hurry."

I looked in the direction of Miriam and Father.

"No one will bother you," he said softly.

I watched him as he left. As on that first day, the sun danced in the chestnut color of his hair. No matter how little I understood some of his actions, I could not feel ill toward Darien. There was something about him that remained innocent and appealing. But I was also afraid. Father and the life he had lived must have left their marks. No one could survive forever the constant reminder of pain such as father must represent to Darien. It was like water dripping on a piece of oak. As hard as the wood was, and however great its resistance, the water would warp the wood, and in the end it would win by its persistence and immutability. Evil, too, would win, for it never varied, never retreated. The persistence of my father's character would eventually kill that innocent quality in Darien.

I wished a new life for him, away from Briarcliff Manor and Miriam and my father.

Darien went up to the house to inspect the chimney. I stood at the crest of the hill and looked at him for a long time. His long legs carried him agilely across the rubble of the fallen walls, and his youthful actions lulled me into thinking of a time long ago, when my mother lived and he had been a happy child. I saw

186

him as she might have, his hair tousled and his face dirty with the perspiration and the dust that only the very young seem to attract in little moist smudges across the bridges of their noses. Perhaps, I thought, this is the true reality of ghosts, that one person can see the hopes and visions that another had, before they failed and died.

For the first time, I had an inkling of what it might mean to be a mother. It brought up in me the most wonderful feelings of hope, and with it a sadness, born out of the sudden thought of Michael. I would probably never know why he had left in such a strange manner, and without so much as a word. There was no one I could turn to who could explain it for me.

Unwilling to pursue this train of thought, I turned away from the sight of Darien and looked at the graves at my feet. I could see from the earth line that he had straightened my mother's headstone from where it had sunk into the earth. The dead stems of a bordering flowerbed waited to be covered by the coming winter snow, and then to be born again with the spring.

It was a long time before I was ready to return to the others. I did not think I could behave normally around father or Miriam ever again. I knew I could not live at Briarcliff Manor with them. Both were evil, twisted people, and I had no weapons to compete with them. I could not be as Darien had been all these years. I did not have the strength to withstand them. I would leave my father to his destiny. I would tell him of what I knew, but I would leave Briarcliff Manor as quickly as I could make arrangements. And this time I would leave without my father's money to use, or a home to return to. Perhaps I would find Michael again someday.

I rose from the bench I had been sitting on, and felt as prepared as I ever could be to face the remainder of the day. As soon as I could I would warn Father of Miriam's intentions, and I would see if I could not convince Darien to leave Briarcliff Manor. Not with me, of course, but to a new life of his own. I had a picture in my mind of him leaving, and I meant to see it happen, if I could. Somehow it felt right to me.

Then, suddenly, I remembered my intentions of helping

my mother come back to life. I had just come home from school then, and I had gone to her room, only to find I was too late. She was already dead. Maybe, now, I could do something for the son of the man she had loved. He was not dead, and for him it might not be too late.

I walked slowly back toward the three of them.

# 15

DARIEN STOOD WITH MY father near the leaning chimney. Father's hand shaded his eyes as he looked up at it.

"That one is in bad shape," he said. "Can you bring it down?"

"Yes, sir," answered Darien with no touch of boastfulness in his voice as he stood swinging the long-handled hammer in his hand. "That's the one Ned told me about. It could fall anytime," he added.

When he saw me, he smiled and came toward me. I glanced over at Miriam busily folding the picnic cloth into a neat little square.

"Do you feel better now?" he asked.

"Yes, I do. Thank you."

I smiled and gave him my hand. We walked together back to where Father stood.

"Can you take it down with that thing?" Father pointed to the hammer Darien still carried in his other hand. "Didn't you bring anything else along?"

He held the heavy instrument before him, the sun glinted off his big squarish head.

"Oh, I think it will do the job," he said. "If it doesn't, I can always find something around here that will."

Father mumbled something and returned to his inspection of the towering chimney. Darien laid the hammer on the ground near Father's feet, and walked appraisingly around the wall again. In spite of its leaning, it was a huge thing for one man to topple. But looking at Darien, I was not in the least uncertain that he would indeed bring it crashing to the ground. As if willing to accept any small victory as a sign of good over evil, I wanted to see the doubt wiped from my father's face.

"Go over there, Annabel," Darien said, indicating a nook in what had been the kitchen. "I don't want you to be hurt."

I looked up at him, questioning. He seemed preoccupied, and answered me distractedly.

"These stones may fly about." He handed me a handkerchief. "Put this over your face. This—the dust may be unpleasant."

I thanked him and backed into the nook he had indicated. He had said nothing to Miriam, but she remained near the picnic basket at the outer edge of the house. She was some distance from the chimney, so I judged her to be safe. Darien carefully removed his coat.

As he stood there in his shirtsleeves and waistcoat, I could not be unaware of the power in his shoulders and back. I thought again what an amazing man he was, and within me my resolution to convince him to begin a new life strengthened. I had often heard that people will not fail when the cause is great enough. I would speak to him as we rode home.

Just as I thought he was going to begin, he came over to where I was waiting.

"Will you get on with this?" Father called out impatiently. "I'm tired. I want to rest. If you can't do the job, say so. I knew you should have brought something else. That hammer is worthless."

"Just a moment, John."

I could hear the restraint in Darien's voice. I wondered how often my father had goaded him, how many times Darien forcibly held himself in check.

"Annabel, I'm sorry," he said as he approached me. "Please believe me. Turn away now."

190

His face had a strange look that brought compassion for him welling up in me. My voice was heavy with my emotions when I replied.

"It's all right. We'll talk later . . . on the way home."

He looked at me for a long time, his eyes sad, but he said nothing aloud. I thought he whispered, "Turn away," but I could not be certain.

Darien picked up the hammer he had laid at Father's feet earlier. He stood very still for a moment, leaning on the handle of the hammer as though it were the only thing in the world that supported him. Then he took a deep breath and the muscles across his back and powerful shoulders flexed as he swung the giant hammer into motion. The cry that came from him was drowned out as I screamed in terror. Father spun in my direction. The hammer blow caught him on the cheekbone, right below his left eye.

His body crumpled lifelessly to the ground like a rag doll's. The heavy head of the hammer had sunk deeply, splintering the bone and the whole side of his face, except for the exposed left eye, which remained intact and staring from the bloody pulp that had been his face.

Darien stood transfixed, his body towering over the still thing that had been my father. He did not say or do anything for some time, and the only sound to come from him was the harsh rasping of his breathing. The world itself seemed to have been put at bay and then hushed by the horror of the scene. It was out of this stillness that the soft mad laughter of Miriam came as she looked into my father's clouding gray eye.

The hammer dropped from Darien's hand. He put his hands up to his face, and his shoulders shook. Then he sprang into action once more. Like a madman he began kicking the body over to the side of the wall by Miriam's feet. He picked up the loose stones on the top of the wall. They were so heavy he had to use both hands to hold them. He raised them one by one over his head, and dropped them down on Father. Over and over his body heaved with the effort as the stones plummeted down over the mass at his feet.

I stood in my corner, choking on my terrified sobs. My

throat felt raw from screaming, yet no sound would come out. It was as though a vise had clamped around my throat, and I could neither speak nor breathe. I tried to shut my eyes and ears from the sounds of Miriam's deathlike cackle and the sight of Darien. I prayed I might faint, but I didn't.

As suddenly as he had begun, he stopped. He wiped his bloody hands on the side of his breeches and went to Miriam. Her hands were clasped before her.

"It's done," she said. "No one will ever know. It's done . . . All of it."

Her face was smiling, and her voice filled with satisfaction. Darien's words came out strange and breathless.

"Give me the bottle."

She looked at him, glanced over at me, and began to fish through her picnic basket. She brought out a small green bottle and handed it to him. He pulled the cork from the bottle with his teeth, and came toward me.

My back was flat to the wall, but I tried frantically to push myself farther away. My feet were in a frenzied battle against the hard surface of the wall behind me, each time slipping down its surface, leaving me exactly where I had been before my attempt at retreat, and Darien moved closer with each useless attempt I made to go nowhere. In spite of the futility, I kept pushing harder against the wall, waves of terror ripping through my stomach and my heart.

I tried to scream, but my throat was paralyzed. He moved slowly toward me, making no attempt at haste, walking without effort. I felt myself growing still and quiet as yet another kind of horror assailed me. His eyes riveted me to the wall as I looked at him. He was looking at me as I had seen him look in the summerhouse when I had thought he loved me. His blood-smeared face had the soft sweet expression that I thought had suited him.

"Annabel."

He said it quietly, barely whispering as he took my hand to his lips.

I remained limp as I felt his moist sticky skin against my hand. I could not make myself react; I stood inert and horror-stricken, unable to block his presence from my consciousness. Why had I not seen any of this in him the night he had frightened me on the terrace? Dear God, it had only been last night.

As though he had read my thoughts, he began to speak again.

"Why wouldn't you come with me?" His hand caressed my face. "I could have left, then. Everything would have turned out the way it should have. You were meant to be mine. It was meant to be that way, and you wouldn't go. Why wouldn't you go with me?"

His hand moved to the back of my neck and loosened my hair, letting it fall over my shoulders. He twined his fingers through it, brushing the long strands against his cheek.

"Michael will never have you. Miriam has taken care of Michael. They'll blame him for all of this."

His voice was calm and empty of emotion. It was as if he were telling me the sun had been shining.

"They'll say he killed John and you, and ran away. Miriam has defeated him." He laughed softly as he looked closely at me, and added. "He'll be hanged for your murder, Annabel."

Then his tone changed sharply and he pulled at my hair harshly. "He wasn't fit to touch you." Mixed with his anger was a kind of childish sorrow. Great tears began to roll down his suntanned face.

"I love you, Annabel. You were meant to be mine."

He stood looking at me, the tears falling and his eyes naked with the pain of years.

"I won't let you be hurt." He held up the bottle he had taken from Miriam. "See, I have brought this. You won't feel anything, Annabel."

Small choking sounds were coming from somewhere inside me.

"Don't be frightened," he said gently.

His eyes traveled from me to the bottle and back again, assuring me that I would not be hurt. He took the handkerchief he had given me from my hand, and poured the vile-smelling liquid from the bottle. He leaned down, kissing me gently on the lips.

"Don't be frightened. I'll put you right beside your mother. And I'll take care of you just like I take care of her. You saw how nice it was up there. I'll always keep it nice. I'll even build your summerhouse and the rose garden, just like I promised. You remember? I said I could always find you there. I'll take care of you. I love you, Annabel."

He kissed my hair and smoothed it back from my face.

"You won't feel the rocks. You'll go to sleep, softly and easily. Annabel, my Annabel."

He spoke my name over and over as he brought the handkerchief to my face. I struggled and fought, finally released from my frozen horror. Around us, as I fought with Darien, the world seemed to be exploding with noise, screaming and shouting, but I could not care about any of it. As I battled desperately for my life, I began to hear a roaring inside my head like the beat of a thousand drums, and the world turned a wavery mixture of gray and green and black moments.

Darien's hand remained fast to my face as my legs gave way. I slithered down the wall to the ground and into blackness. It felt so good to finally be free of the horror—if only the roaring in my head would stop. I felt a sharp pain in my back, and then a great weight pressing in against me.

I could still feel the weight pressing on me, and I could feel warmth. Dead people were cold. I was warm. I wasn't dead. I would not open my eyes. I was afraid he would see I wasn't dead, and put that thing over my face again. And then came the horrible thought: maybe it wasn't over. He said I wouldn't feel anything. He said I wouldn't feel the rocks. But I could feel. I was warm.

The weight moved and I nearly opened my eyes. But I didn't. I prayed he'd think me dead, then he wouldn't do anything. He was still there, I knew it, I could feel it. His voice was there saying Annabel over and over, insistent, trying to trick me into opening my eyes, trying to make me come back. And his tears . . . they were falling on me. I would stay closed away here, inside myself. The horror of it all seemed less real as it whizzed around in the darkness of my mind. I did not want to see, but his voice kept calling, Annabel . . . Annabel . . . Annabel . . . pulling at me so I could not fight.

I squeezed my eyes tightly, trying to keep them shut, trying to remain safe in the blackness. When I opened them, I looked up into the great dark pools of Michael's eyes.

I think I finally fainted, for I do not remember anything but Michael's eyes. Later, when I opened my eyes again, I was safely snug in his arms.

"Michael?" I whispered, trying to be certain it was really he. He held me closer.

"Annabel, you're all right! Thank God. I thought I had lost you." He kissed me and pulled me closer against him. "I thought I was too late. But you are all right. You *are*, aren't you?"

"Yes, I am, but—"

"I know, don't think of it."

He began to stir.

"Michael, don't!" I cried, frightened again. "Darien will find us. Don't move. He's—"

He ran his hand gently over my hair. "He can't harm you now."

"No, Michael, you don't understand. He's mad. They both . . . came here to . . . and Miriam was laughing and laughing."

I had begun to choke again, and I was trembling all over. He pulled me close against him once more.

"No, Annabel, Darien won't harm you. He's dead."

"Miriam?"

He jerked his head to the side. "She is over there."

"Dead?"

"No, but she won't do anything to you or to anyone else. Can you get up?"

"I don't know."

He lifted me into his arms and set me in the carriage.

As I looked about me, I saw the wreckage of this day. Father lay beneath a huge pile of stone. The house was a powdering mass of settling dust. Only three of the walls remained standing. The others had fallen. Somewhere beneath them lay Darien. Miriam had been lucky, as had Michael and I—she had not been hit by some of the stones as the house collapsed but she was alive.

I was the only one, as Darien had promised, who had not felt the stones. As Michael walked back to get Miriam, I saw that he too had been hurt. He was the weight that had fallen on me, and all of the rocks that should have pelted down on me had hit him.

At the time I did not even consider why he was there, or where he had come from. I only thanked God that he was.

He came back to the carriage, carrying Miriam. From what source he drew his strength I shall never know, for I could see the strain in his face as he returned with her in his arms. His breathing was heavy and his movements now showed the pain he felt. We returned to Briarcliff Manor, a bloodied and spent trio. Matthew's frantic appraisal brought the entire staff out into the courtyard or racing to the windows to see what had caused the commotion.

The confusion about us was indescribable, each of them trying in some way to help, and trying to find out what had happened. Ernest and Jacobs carried Miriam to her room. Matthew sent one of the grooms for Dr. Schwartz, and another to return the horse Michael had borrowed from a neighbor to ride out to the ruin.

Michael was sitting in the driver's seat of the carriage, perfectly calm, directing the people around us. I stayed by his side, motionless in my seat. I refused to allow anyone to take me from it. When Michael alit I scrambled down before anyone could assist me and ran to him. He put his arm around my waist, and with a nonsensical sense of relief I heard him give orders to Lettie to lock the unconscious Miriam in her room.

Soon after, we went into the house. Aggie and Lettie, now returned, were clucking at me to go to my room to rest until the doctor came. I clung desperately to Michael, his coat crumpled securely in my fist. I was terrified to leave his side, and I hated them all for trying to pry me loose. I wanted them to go away and let me be with him.

Michael didn't say a word, but took me to my room. He opened the door with his free hand, then looked back over his shoulder at Lettie and Aggie, who had followed us. Silently they left, and Michael closed the door behind us. We went into the sitting room. I don't believe we spoke a word. I don't remember any. We sat huddled together for a long while, and we fell asleep.

Dr. Schwartz had not been easy to find, so it was quite late when Lettie came upstairs to fetch us. Michael had heard her knocking at the door before I had, and he gently shook me by the shoulder to awaken me. For a moment I could not get my bearings. I thought I was back at the ruin. He held me close, reassuring me as Lettie's persistent knock continued.

"Don't you think I had better let her in?" he said. "She will be imagining all sorts of things."

I nodded but did not release my grip on him.

He smiled and said, "You know, don't you, you are forcing me to marry you."

I released him and said stupidly, "Oh, Michael! Would you?"

His laughter fell like a bright shining moment across the horrible day.

"Lettie, come in," he called out.

He observed none of the amenities. He stayed seated by my side, holding me close. Lettie was both relieved and embarrassed as she beheld the sight of two very dirty, very improper people before her. Her voice clearly showed her mixture of impressions as she delivered her message.

"Dr. Schwartz is here, Mr. . . . Miss . . . Annabel."

She turned quickly and scurried out the door.

Dr. Schwartz pronounced me fit and unharmed. Michael he chased to bed. Jacobs and Ernest were ordered to sit on him if necessary, but to keep him there. I did not tell the doctor, but I had every intention of tending to Michael myself. There was nothing seriously wrong with him, and Michael protested furiously, but he finally gave up in defeat.

Miriam, I was told, would recover. I did not want to hear about her, and so Dr. Schwartz did not press me with details. He told me only that she had been struck on the head, and, he believed, would recover handily from that. Otherwise, she was badly bruised.

Dr. Schwartz went downstairs, where Jacobs and Matthew

waited to see him out. He had displayed admirable restraint with Michael and me, asking us few questions about the circumstances that caused us all to be in such a condition. As I stood near the head of the stairs, I heard the dam of his curiosity burst as soon as he spied Matthew and Jacobs.

"What has happened here today? Am I to understand John Arbriar is dead, and Darien Varka as well?"

I do not know why I wanted to stand there and overhear the conversation, but I did. Perhaps it made the whole affair seem finished to hear others speak of it in tones of curiosity and unreality. They had not lived it, and their voices carried none of the horrors of living and seeing it.

"That is what Mr. Barington said," Jacobs replied.

Matthew, never as reticent as Jacobs, had just had a report from the groom he had sent after Michael's horse.

"If Mr. Barington said they are dead," he said, "you can rest your life on it that it is true. He has been watching things around here for some time."

His voice was proud as he continued. "I have been helping him myself. When Mr. Darien meddled with Miss Annabel's horse, it was him and me that found it out. And I was the one helped him plan his moves today."

Matthew stopped talking, I suppose to let the full importance of what he said sink into the minds of his listeners. I had no idea where Michael had been those two days he had disappeared, and I hadn't asked him. Nor had I known that Darien had been responsible for Bucephalus' strange and erratic fear of jumping. Moving closer so I could see as well as hear, I sat down on the steps. I didn't think they could see me from where they stood, but I really didn't care.

Dr. Schwartz was saying that Michael had spoken to him about Miriam at the time John became ill.

"Of course, I thought the man was exaggerating his worries," he said. "One hardly expects an acquaintance to be a murderess. But what happened today, what brought all this on?"

"Mr. Barington stayed away from the house for the past two days. Mrs. Arbriar had given him a date to be gone, so he let her think he was doing as she asked. Most of the time he stayed with me in the stables—"

Dr. Schwartz broke in impatiently. "Get on with it, man! We know he counted on you. Very admirable, I'm sure. But what happened?"

Matthew looked hurt.

"Well, I don't know exactly. All I know is what Ned told me when he came back from old Jenkins' stable."

I started to leave, expecting no more from him. Then he said, "Mr. Barington put Miss Clarissa on a train for the east, and raced like a madman, old Jenkins said, for the stable. He said he never saw a man in such a hurry. He took the first horse he saw, and jumped on its back, no saddle or nothing. Jenkins was fit to be tied, it was his best horse, and Mr. Barington didn't say nothing to him, just came in like a bull and run off with his horse."

Matthew's face took on an amused, confidential look.

"Mr. Barington told Miss Annabel he hired that horse, but you should hear old Jenkins tell it. Jenkins says he tore out of the stable, getting that horse to give as much as he had in him. People scattered all over the street. That man weren't going to stop for no one. He headed right out of town back to Briarcliff Manor and the old ruin, riding like the furies were on his tail."

"Then what?" asked Dr. Schwartz.

"I don't know what. Something happened out there."

"For God's sake, man! I know something happened. Why didn't you tell me you didn't know what it was?"

With that retort, Dr. Schwartz smashed his hat on his head and slammed out the front door, leaving Matthew and Jacobs standing at the foot of the stairs. They looked at each other, perplexed.

"We had better buy that horse from Jenkins," Matthew said. He waited for Jacobs to say something. When he did not, Matthew added as though in apology, "That horse ain't fit for the glue pot now. Mr. Barington run his legs to little bitty stubs."

Jacobs said something in reply, but I could not catch it, as they were moving away in the direction of the kitchen. I would have wagered their destination was the brandy cabinet. They could have it all, and with my blessing. I was bursting with pride for Michael.

For the two days that Michael was confined to his room, a steady stream of people came and went. Dr. Schwartz was very attentive, and returned the following afternoon. I noticed he stayed longer with Michael than was necessary for a mere examination, and he did not seek information from anyone else that day. I surmised he finally had the whole story.

Neither Michael nor I knew exactly where Father's or Darien's bodies were. Nothing had been left to identify when most of the walls and the chimney had crashed to the ground. Michael had to send Ned and some of the other men digging through the ruins to find them. They returned to Michael's room and reported the discovery of the two bodies.

Michael never did tell me how he had come back to Briarcliff Manor that day. Like Dr. Schwartz, I was forced to get bits and pieces of it from the servants whenever I could find one who had not already been warned by Michael not to upset me. All I was able to discover was that he had ridden up as I was struggling with Darien. I suppose that had been the noise and the shouting I had heard. Miriam had screamed and run for the hammer when she saw Michael. She had tried to hit him with it, but fortunately it proved too heavy for her to handle.

Michael had pulled Darien away from me. They had fought. One of them had the hammer, and I never wanted to know which one it was. They had moved up near the chimney. In their struggle they loosed the crumbling foundation of the wall and it began to topple, bringing the chimney with it.

Michael had run and dived over me. Darien either did not see what was happening, or simply stayed there to let it happen. The chimney started the other walls falling, and he was trapped as the walls came down on him.

I did not tell Michael what I had found out. To this day, he tries to protect me from those memories. But I learned that it is not wise to be ignorant of what goes on around you. Perhaps much of this tragedy would not have happened had I known the circumstances of life as they truly were at Briarcliff Manor.

In those first few days after the tragedy, as I watched Michael give his orders to the men, all the while remembering never to say anything he felt might remind me of Darien or Father, I marveled that such a man as he would one day be my husband. I obliged him in every way I could. I asked no questions of him, nor did I show in any way that I knew what he spoke of when he talked to the men in oblique fashion about the arrangements that had to be made. To him I spoke only of happy things, and took care of him. I remember it as one of the most peaceful times of my life.

Then, the first day Michael was again up and around, we went to the funeral for Father and Darien. Both of them were buried in the south field plot near the house beside Darien's father and my mother. It seemed the only place for them, and somehow, I thought they would want to be there. Perhaps in some life hereafter they would sort out the wicked and tragic things they had done to one another.

Later that same day, I resolved to question Michael. Now that he was recovered, I did not want any secrets between us. I already knew what Michael would tell me, but I wanted it open between ourselves and not from others' lips. Now that it was all over, Michael was slowly becoming his old exasperating self. In spite of the fact that most of his teasing was directed at me, I was happy to see this trait return. He had been all seriousness while he dealt with the problems of the two funerals, and the painful and complicated matter of Miriam. The police investigators were very reassuring about the conclusion to the mystery of Charles Asherton's death. It was a near-certainty that Miriam would be held responsible for that as well. Little by little, the last remaining influences that Miriam and my father had exerted on those about them were being destroyed.

So when Michael returned from taking Miriam into town with the police, I was anxiously awaiting the moment when we could talk. He came through the door, looking tired and serious. After we had eaten lunch we walked out into the garden. He took deep breaths, as though trying to bring new life and freshness into himself. It was too cold to be comfortable, so we went into the library, where Jacobs had started a fire.

We gathered up the few throw pillows in the room and settled down on the hearth. I could not go any longer without asking him my questions.

"Michael, where did you go that morning I thought you had left?"

He looked at me, his expression totally serious.

"I tried to run off with Clarissa, but she wouldn't have me."

"Michael!"

He assured me he hadn't meant a word he said, and I enjoyed letting him worry that I had believed him. Then, I asked him how he knew Miriam had that day in mind to kill my father and me.

"I didn't," he said. "It just seemed like a good possibility."

"It was, but do you know why?"

"No, do you?"

"Yes," I replied. "Miriam wanted the murders to happen on the day you left, so that it would seem as though you had killed father and me and then run away. People would think you had killed your uncle as well. And she'd have Darien to back up her claims."

He sat still for a moment, looking into the fire.

"It would have worked," he said finally. "There would have been no one left to say otherwise, except for me, of course. I doubt my word would have carried much weight."

We were both quiet for a long while. Thoughts of Miriam and her plans often left one speechless. I could never think of her without ending my efforts with a feeling of emptiness and sorrow. Finally I turned to Michael.

"What would you have done if she *hadn't* done anything that day?"

"First, I would have looked quite a fool riding out there as I did, and then I would have stayed out of sight until Matthew told me something was going on."

"Do you mean you were going to let me think you had walked right out of my life until Miriam did something awful? No matter how long it took?"

"Um—humm." He grinned.

"You could have at least told me."

202

He was still grinning as he shrugged his shoulders in reply.

"You were just going to let me *wait*, Michael!"

"You have no patience, no trust," he said. "But since you don't, we'll be married this weekend."

He patted my hand, as though the matter were settled.

"This weekend? In three days? . . . But the period of mourning. What will people think?"

He looked at me. "The same thing Lettie is already thinking. It had better be this weekend. You don't think I can stay here otherwise, do you? I have my good name to think of. What would people say?"

I picked up the little pillow from behind my back and threw it at him. He rushed out of the room, calling back to me.

"You'll make a shrewish wife! People will say they pity me, that's what they'll say."

Michael and I were married as quietly as possible. But in all my dreams of beautiful weddings, I had never imagined one better than ours. We returned late to Briarcliff Manor Sunday evening, as we had planned. When we rode toward the towering stone house we saw the windows shining with the candlelight from within. It looked as though a great party was going on inside.

Matthew came round in front and took the carriage for Michael. We thanked him, and he had just climbed into the driver's seat when the front door burst wide. All the servants of Briarcliff Manor spilled from the door to greet us. I was both pleased and concerned as I saw them rush out. Michael would never run a proper household; no one at the Manor would ever again know he had a "place" to keep. What *would* the neighbors think of my rollicking crew?

As I was being hugged and patted and congratulated by friends who before had barely spoken to me unless given permission, I decided not to worry about the neighbors. I fell in with the lively gaiety of the others. Michael had no problems fitting in at all. He danced with every woman in the house, young and old, and joked and hooted with every man.

As the festivities began to wind to a close, each person came to us in imitation of the formality they had seen at other Briarcliff Manor parties. They all welcomed us home, and told Michael they would look forward to next year's party, which I gathered Michael had determined to make an annual affair.

Aggie was the last to come to us. She gave me a great hug.

"You'll be happy now, miss," she said, then clapped her hand to her mouth and looked at Michael. "I mean Mrs. Barington!" She smiled up at him, and then looked back to me. "Briarcliff Manor has a good master now."

She went off, and I dreamily looked about the now empty room.

"What are you thinking?" Michael asked.

"Briarcliff Manor is a very different place now."

"Yes," he said. "Do you mind if we change the name?"

"There is no briar in your name," I said.

"No, there isn't."

"There is no briar in *my* name, Michael."

"No."

"Barington!"

He smiled and took me in his arms. And then, Michael and I went hand in hand upstairs to spend our first night in Barington Hall.